His gaze stopped on a woman sitting alone in the booth at the far left corner.

She wore Hammarleeding garb – wool tunic and leggings like his – hers drab in subdued ecru decorated by patterns of gray and white. She was bony, rangy, likely quite tall . . . and she held herself like a queen, straight and graceful as she sipped her cup of tea.

The frontiersmen began a rollicking ballad about bears dancing in the woods, and the Hammarleeding woman turned her face toward them.

Ivvar felt all the air punch out of his lungs.

Also by J.M. Ney-Grimm

WINTER GLORY

KAUNIS CLAN SAGA

by J.M. Ney-Grimm

Wild
Unicorn

ISBN-13: 978-0692438251
ISBN-10: 0692438254

Designed by JMNG

Cover art:
"So the man gave him a pair of snow-shoes" by Kay Nielsen
(black & white rendition by J.M. Ney-Grimm)

Interior illustration:
"American Larch" by Stefen Bernath
"Woodwork Frame" from the Dover Pictorial Archive series

In memory of
Papa,
calm like warm sunlight

WINTER GLORY

His stomach felt curiously hollow. For no reason at all that he could discern.

Ivvar stood to one side of the wide doorway, appreciating the din of hearty men in converse over their noontime meal. So like the rumbling tones of his brothers back home in the refecting-hall of Rakas-lodge. Except these were lowlanders in a lowland village guesthouse on the edge of the vast northern pine forests, not mountain men in an enclave of the high Fiordhammars.

The trappers in their fringed buckskin jackets and pants were in from the woods, waiting for the season to turn from late winter to spring, and the arctic foxes to complete their change from white pelts to red. The loggers, sporting plaid wool jackets and bushy beards, would be gone the instant the rivers shook free of old rotten ice and flowed unhindered, ready to float ponderous pine trunks east to the sawmills. A few ice men in their neutral patterned knit sweaters, reluctant perhaps to return to their farms in the south, enjoyed a last flagon of ale with their friends. Their brutal work of hacking massive cubes of ice from the frozen lakes of the region was over.

Good cheer and robust camaraderie filled the generous space to its rafters and its peeled log walls, the warm gold of old pine.

No reason at all in this warm room full of vigorous conviviality for an echo of old grief to chill Ivvar's belly.

He'd come straight from the bath house, following a narrow corridor from the back of the inn through to its front hall. Almost like a bee moving between walls of golden honeycomb, save for the vivid stencils of red and white and blue diamond shapes that adorned the pine paneling above the chair rail.

His joints had felt loose and warm from the sauna, and from his morning's stint of cross-country skiing, the final short leg of his journey before he reached the porch of the Mink and Mug. No old man's bones for him. Not yet. Even though he was an old man, pushing ninety in another three years. And his hair showed it: shoulder-length dreadlocks of gray streaked with white.

He'd chosen his summer weight tunic and leggings – sage green wool, traced by soft blue designs – knowing the lowlanders kept their buildings hotter than did the mountain folk. He'd remained slipperless for the same reason. The wide pine boards of the floor felt smooth under his bare feet. Well-swept by the staff, evidently.

The proprietress kept a clean house.

The smells of the luncheon would have led him straight to the dining hall, if he'd not already known where to find it. Fragrant buckwheat flapjacks, sweet lingonberry syrup, and rich sausages, threaded by a yeasty hint of ale and the meaty savor of a stew.

But, over it all, the amazing fragrance of baking rye bread.

He drew in a long breath. The food of his mountain home featured few grains. And Ivvar had developed a taste for fresh bread in his lowland travels.

Almost did the aroma of the baking loaves settle the quiver in his belly as he surveyed the room, its long pine tables and benches crowded by rowdy frontiersmen, its cylindrical tile stove – blue and white – radiating heat from its center. A row of square window casements punctuated the far wall, their small circular panes permitting a wavery view of gray sky and snowy pines outside. Wooden booths on a raised level around the edge of the space, one step up from the main floor, provided a few guests a more private meal than could be had at the communal tables.

Ivvar scanned these diners. Mostly holiday lowlanders visiting the back country, he'd guess.

No, not quite.

His gaze stopped on a woman sitting alone in the booth at the far left corner.

She wore Hammarleeding garb – wool tunic and leggings like his – hers drab in subdued ecru decorated by patterns of gray and white. She was bony, rangy, likely quite tall when she stood. And old, like him. She'd pinned her long iron-gray braid around her head like a coronet, and she held herself like a queen, straight and graceful as she sipped her cup of tea.

The frontiersmen began a rollicking ballad about bears dancing in the woods, and the Hammarleeding woman turned her face toward them.

Ivvar felt all the air punch out of his lungs.

She wasn't beautiful, but she drew him. Lightly tanned skin like his own; straight nose, a little on the long side; flat cheeks. Laugh lines framed her firm mouth. Crow's feet bordered her level hazel eyes. He suspected she'd reached that calm place where life was just interesting, neither a tragedy to be resisted, nor a passion to be exalted. But what was it about her . . . ?

She looked genuine and . . . appealing.

The flutter in his innards grew.

Then lagging memory brought another face before his mind's eye.

Like to the one across the room from him in the here-and-now. So like. But younger; fifty or more years younger. Jaw clenched, hazel eyes hot, and lips tight with anger. His linking-sister – what these lowlanders would call his wife. His former wife. Paiam.

The last time he'd seen her, angry at life itself more than at him, but telling him their linking – their marriage – must end.

How had she grown into this serene old grandmother?

For this was Paiam, he had no doubt. None at all. His linking-sister herself, some fifty years down the road, some fifty years wiser by the look of her.

As he watched her, a twinkle came into her eyes, and her wool-slippered foot tapped to the rhythm of the frontiersmen's song.

Ivvar shifted his weight forward onto his toes to go to her, then abruptly swung around to seek the stairs up to his bednook.

No. He wouldn't approach her.

He'd left Tukeva-lodge to make his home in Rakas all those years ago, because seeing Paiam while no longer linked to her was too painful. Their love had never cooled. The end of their linking had never been about love's lack. Nor even fundamental differences. Nothing so simple.

And, away from her, he'd found his peace.

It looked as though she had too.

He would not disturb her. Or himself any more than the sight of her had done.

A slight smile twitched his lips as he set his foot to the first step on the staircase up, felt the polished bannister under his hand. The flex in his thigh muscles as he climbed reminded him of the steepness of the path approaching Kaunis-lodge, Paiam's home. But he wouldn't think of that either. It was all so very long ago.

He'd taken an actual room in the guesthouse rather than one of the bednooks behind the cupboard doors that lined the upper hallways. His room had a bednook, of course: a paneled cabinet just the size of the mattress with enough headroom for him to sit up in it. One of the nooks along the corridor would have been more like home, but most lowlander inns featured rooms for their bednooks, and he'd grown accustomed to the luxury as he traveled north.

His door stood open. One of the chambermaids had been sweeping the floor in his room, but she'd abandoned her broom to examine his unusual cloak.

Was she newly hired?

Perhaps she'd not encountered a Hammarleeding before. No other people in the North-lands wore hoods fashioned from the heads of beasts. His own garment, a black wolf's pelt complete with the fur-covered skull forming its headpiece, hung on a hook just inside the door; rough and scarred and sinister. He'd killed the beast when he was a young man, when it was his job to protect the flocks of Tukeva-lodge and their young shepherds from the *onderneming*, those fierce beasts who hunted the mountains in winter – frost leopards, north-bears, ice tigers . . . and wolves. The predator that became his cloak had been a canny old patriarch with a taste for human flesh.

The chamber maid's hand darted away as Ivvar stepped into the room.

"Were you curious, child?" He could tell she hadn't thievery in mind.

"Oh!" she gasped, eyes round, hands twisting in her red and white striped apron. "I do be so sorry, herralte!"

He still wasn't used to the lowlander honorific "high sir." But it behoved him to reassure the girl. She reminded him a little of his great granddaughter: inquisitive, open to wonder, and not mindful of the proprieties. Although little Tapat was considerably younger, just four years to this child's fifteen or sixteen.

"Does not your patter or your brother wear wool against the chill in winter?" The lowlanders called their fathers "patter" and their mothers "motter."

"Sheepskin, herralte." She was still rattled; knew she shouldn't have been prying into a guest's belongings; likely found the glinting glass eyes of the wolf "hood" appalling.

"The winter storms of my mountains bring a cold more bitter than those of your lowlands. This wolfskin holds warmth to me, even in gusting winds." As well it should, imbued with *duoja* – what the lowlanders might call keyholding or magic – by his own skilled fingertips.

"I do be so sorry, herralte," she repeated, glancing nervously at the door behind him, clearly longing to go. "I meant no harm!"

Perhaps he should scold her, but he judged she'd learned an important lesson. He'd be kind and turn her attention. Some lowlanders would always be unnerved by Hammarleeding ways, no matter how often they encountered them. He had a meal to order.

"Will you carry my luncheon request to the kitchen, child? I've a fancy to dine here in my room."

"Oh, yes, herralte," she assured him. "Maitresse Odissa expects the chamber maids to wait on her guests, not just to tidy and clean." Her gaze dropped, caught on his bare feet, and flew back to his face. "Your toes will freeze, herralte!"

Ivvar laughed. "No, the guesthouse is overly hot were I to don short-hose and boots. I prefer to do my sweating in the sauna, not here."

She giggled, her anxiety temporarily forgotten. He told her the dishes he wanted before she had time to remember her fears.

He checked his gear once she was gone. Leather pack leaning unopened against the wall under his cloak, brushed by its lowest folds. A tumble of sweaty traveling clothes, boiled wool boots, belt, mitts, and canteen just as he'd left them. No, she was honest, as he'd thought.

He moved to the casement window on the outer wall.

His room followed the pattern for all the guest chambers in The Mink and Mug: square with a columnar tile stove on an inner corner, a small round table with two wooden chairs in an outer corner, a built-in bednook – just like those along the hall, doors closed – along one side wall, and a double-hinged casement window letting in a flood of pale, cloudy light. All the woodwork glowed the same golden hue of old pine found throughout the inn, but the stencils in this room were blue and green and white, while the base color of the table and chairs was orange-red paint. Another difference from home, where the furnishings retained the blonds and reds and browns of their natural wood.

The casement itself provided a more striking difference. Hammarleeding lodges secured their windows with stretched hides. They let light in, but gave no view out. While the Reindeer People, where his granddaughter and her children lived, and to whom he was traveling, were nomadic and their tents possessed no windows at all.

But lowlanders, ah – they used glass as though it were water: nearly a hundred small circular panes in this one window of the many in The Mink and Mug.

Glass windows would remain a wonder to him no matter how many times he traveled the lowlands.

This one featured exceptionally clear panes showing an unblurred panorama beyond: the snowy road he'd skied north on winding between thickets of spruce and pine across fairly flat terrain. The hilly regions were farther south.

The Mink and Mug lay on the edge of its tiny hamlet. The neighboring blacksmith, livery, and sleigh-maker were all located on the other side of the guesthouse, not visible from his chamber; not cluttering his view of the natural landscape.

Cold seeped in through the bronze fittings of the casement. Ivvar touched his fingers to the smooth metal. His room was cooler than the halls and common areas of The Mink and Mug, gratefully so to his preferences. His instructions to let the coals die down in the tile stove had been followed – good – but it would be some hours before the masonry behind the decorative tiles let go its excessive warmth. The cold window felt nice.

The food tasted equally so when it arrived: savory sausages, sweet pear preserves, salty turnip ferment, and best of all, slice after slice of toasted rye bread slathered in butter and washed down by pungent apple kvass.

His mountain folk occasionally hunted the wild snow pigs, but the uplands were too severe for the fat, domestic pigs kept by the lowlanders. Nor did apples grow in the high valleys. Nor rye. One of the pleasures of wandering and roaming, if you owned an adventurous palate, was the foreign comestibles.

Ivvar chuckled softly. Paiam had not shared his love of unfamiliar tastes.

He felt gloriously replete upon finishing his luncheon, but the room remained overly warm.

He rummaged in his pack for a knob of spruce gum. He chose a fresh piece, hard and crumbly, the way it was at first, but with a burst of freshness so strong as to make it harsh. It would get smooth and sweet after he chewed it a while, and it chased the lingering food tastes from his tongue. He preferred a clean mouth.

Then he pulled on some short-hose and his boots, locked his door, lounged down to the front of The Mink and Mug, and went out.

One of the holiday couples occupied a bench on the front veranda, well bundled in furs and hats, but sitting close and talking softly.

He left them to their private chat, passing down the veranda steps and on into the adjacent woods. He walked until he couldn't hear the tinking sound drifting from the blacksmith's or the shouts of the ostlers at the livery or the hearty laugh of the sledwright's son.

The cloud cover thinned enough to bring a pattern of dapple and light on the rough pine trunks and the thin snow cover. He found a particularly large tree with high branches and a spread of dry pine needles under its shelter. He lowered his long self to the ground and leaned back against the bark. It dug into his shoulderblades pleasantly. He'd not bothered with either his thistlesilk jacket or his cloak. The afternoon was merely pleasantly cool to him. He tipped his head back, feeling the wool of his hair catch on the tree's texture. He cracked his gum. And thought.

Lowlander families were structured so peculiarly. Husband and wife lived in the same house following their marriage, and all the children from their union lived with them until they reached adulthood. The eldest daughter eventually inherited the farm, if they owned one, and many lowlanders did. The rest of the young struck off on their own. And Silmaren was big, with many frontier lands calling out for settlers.

But the way Hammarleedings arranged things was utterly different from the lowlanders.

A man lived with all his clan-brothers – the whole mob of them, not just his siblings – in the father-lodge. Ivvar's home had been Tukeva-lodge.

Ivvar grinned, remembering a time when he was very small and the brothers had invented a tumbling game to amuse themselves and their youngest sons. It was winter, and the snow was deep and soft. How he'd flown through the air, a tucked ball of delighted toddler, tossed from man to man. The ride ended with him dunked in a fluffy pile shoveled up for the purpose, laughing. The sisters would never have allowed it.

But Hammarleeding women lived with their clan-sisters in the mother-lodge, so they'd known nothing about that game or any of the other rough fun the brothers devised.

Paiam's home was Kaunis-lodge, the sister-lodge where the brothers of Tukeva-lodge visited to celebrate Hammarleeding holy days. It was at Kaunis that the linking ceremonies were performed – the lowlanders would call them marriages. In the Kaunis calling hall, he'd linked with Paiam, glorying in her happy radiance.

From the time he'd grown old enough to think of such things, he'd hoped to link with Paiam. He'd loved the clear, strong tone of her voice when she called to her sisters on the slopes outside during the biannual herd-luring rite. The lanky grace of her body when she ran. The assurance in her demeanor.

He'd been cautious in his courtship. She had a temper, he knew. She could be unexpectedly prickly. It would never do to get off on the wrong foot. He wouldn't get a second chance.

But, as it happened, she'd had her eye on him. She'd hoped he would approach her. After their linking, she'd confessed that she'd always loved his "gentle strength" and been prickly because she was sure he preferred more demure girls.

No, he hadn't preferred demure girls. Or any other girls. It had always been Paiam. It always would be Paiam.

Except their linking did not last.

Some brothers and sisters preferred a limited linking. Just enough to conceive children, and then the couple parted. But Ivvar had planned to remain linked with Paiam until the end of his days. And she had felt the same. Which made it all the more painful when their linking broke.

Hammarleeding couples didn't live together the way lowlanders did, but the romantic legend of Aila and Bierran – faithful lovers in the ancient past – inspired many a brother to love his lady to the end of time. Ivvar had hoped to rival Bierran in his steadfastness.

He flashed again to that long ago day when Paiam told him that it was over. "Stay away from me, Ivvar Dainar-spring," she'd said, that usually clear voice of hers low and tense and angry. "If I am standing in the front of the hall, you stand at the back. If I am dining at a table near the windows in the refectory, you dine at one near the kitchens. If I dance high on the slope during the herd luring, you do so on the downslope. I won't have you ruining my life!"

Her face had been just as tense and angry as her voice.

He'd done her one better. Made Rakas-lodge his home and celebrated the holy days with its sister-lodge, Illoiset. He'd never seen her again.

Until today.

He scooped up a handful of pine needles, cold and almost silky along their lengths, prickly on the ends – like Paiam – and let them drift through his fingers back to the ground. The pitchy scent of the tree at his back surrounded him. The spruce gum in his mouth had grown soft and sweet with chewing.

Should he have approached Paiam earlier in the dining hall of The Mink and Mug?

He knew why she was here, of course.

Their granddaughter Livli – the one who had left the mountains to live amongst the Reindeer People – had given birth to a fourth child, a daughter, a few months ago.

The estrangement between Ivvar and Paiam had not extended to a breach involving their descendants. Their daughter, Sarvet, had sought Ivvar the moment she emerged from Paiam's rather domineering authority. And Livli, Sarvet's daughter, had visited Ivvar regularly throughout her childhood.

Paiam was undoubtedly going to see the new great grandchild. As was he.

Sheer chance that they had picked the same time.

No, he was glad he'd not approached her. He'd stick by that decision.

She is better without me. And I? That was a more complex answer.

It would be inconvenient once they both reached the ambit of the nomadic Reindeer tribe, but they'd manage. There were three other great grandchildren who would benefit from some extra attention. After fifty some years, he and Paiam were surely capable of civility during the brief encounters that would come while living within Minmahal-tribe, and the rest of the time they could divide however it worked best. He would manage.

No, he would do more than manage. He would avoid Paiam here in The Mink and Mug. But once within Minmahal-tribe, he would seek her out and determine the terms of their interaction. Not leave things to chance.

Yes.

A breeze stirred the still air.

Ivvar climbed back to his feet. He'd walk through the forest for a while, then return to the inn for a short nap, and eat supper in his room.

～

Ivvar lingered in The Mink and Mug the next morning, determined to make a late start, which felt odd since he preferred early ones. But Paiam had always been an early riser herself, and he wanted to delay their encounter until his arrival amongst the Reindeer People. Traveling together . . .

No. No, that wouldn't work at all. He suppressed a derisive grin.

The Mink and Mug was an easy place to loiter, especially now that his room had cooled sufficiently to be comfortable. He did his usual dawn branching sequence, a series of stretches and poses that soothed his achy joints and calmed his mind, then continued with some advanced postures that he'd skipped while skiing north.

He found himself wobbling on the half-moon pose, balanced on his left leg while tipped sideways with his torso and right leg parallel to the floor, his arms straight out from his shoulders, one pointing up, the other reaching down toward the floor. His long limbs generated a lot of unbalancing leverage.

He drew in a deeper than ordinary breath and slowly exhaled, feeling steadiness return. That was better. Clearly half-moon needed to be part of his regular routine.

He broke his fast with a large meal: rye porridge and salt ham, fermented onion, herring in vinegar, mint tea, and cloudberry preserves. Lowland food was so filling. But still he couldn't get enough of the stuff.

He'd arranged for the services of the laundress the day before, so his clothes were clean and folded, but he'd not loaded his pack. Deliberately. Nor had he organized storage for his skis and poles here at The Mink and Mug.

The snow cover had lasted long enough for him to ski this far, but the bare patches in the forest showed that skiing wouldn't be feasible much longer. He'd cache his skis and continue on snowshoes.

Maitresse Odissa had kept his skis before when he visited Livli, returning them to him when he journeyed home again.

As he expected, she was happy to oblige this time as well.

He checked over his gear. He'd done it before he left Rakas-lodge of course. But a man couldn't be too prepared when penetrating the backcountry.

The lowlands of Silmaren were dotted over with orchards, sheep meadows, farm hillcots, and hamlets. The farther north one went, the sparser the presence of people, but there was help available in emergency. Perhaps too late and too little, but there.

In the backcountry . . . league after league of pine forests, spruce barrens, and chains of lakes, with only a few timber mills and fisheries. The wilds were wide and people absent from most of them. Especially during the turnover when trappers and loggers were awaiting the change of the season, and the ice men were done with their labors.

If Ivvar encountered trouble, he'd need to handle it himself.

He pulled out his hunting knife and scrutinized it. Blade oiled and honed. Grip wrappings secure and firm. Scabbard seams strong and intact.

The knife had stayed in his pack up to now. But wolves and north-bears and other predators roamed the northwest. Stalked by an ice tiger last year, Ivvar had drawn on his old skills from when he'd hunted the *onderneming* as a youth in the Fiordhammars of the Hammarleedings. He would be ready this time too. For whatever.

Stowing and arranging everything took some time, and then he could bear to wait no longer. If he were a mere four hours behind Paiam, so be it. A couple hours before the noontide, he made his departure, lifting a hand to Maittresse Odissa, who stepped onto the veranda to see him off.

The overcast spread high and thin, thinner than yesterday, almost sunny. The snow on the road held a warmth to its whiteness, and the forest floor flanking it showed dappled textures beneath the tall pine boles. A bird called, soft and clear: *twoo woo*. A faint stirring of the still air rustled the pine needles. Ivvar loved the cool freshness of the outdoors.

He settled into the rhythm of snowshoeing, a brisk walk, less smooth than the skiing which he preferred, but with a similar motion in the toes, bending at the ball of the foot to slide the back shoe forward, flattening the foot to take his weight. He'd modified the traditional design of his snowshoes, making them narrower than most and a bit longer to compensate for the loss of width. His height gave him weight to match. The shoes needed enough area to support him on soft snow. His modification meant the inner edges needn't slide over one another as he moved, allowing him a bit more speed. He liked speed.

He'd strapped his wolf cloak to the top flap of his pack and donned a very light silk jacket – muted blue, trapunto quilted, and with tie-on sleeves removed.

The day was too mild for heavy layers, and the jacket would cut the wind generated by his movement. The trapunto work on the jacket was his own, imbued with *duoja* to improve the wind-blocking qualities of the garment. He'd used a spiral pattern to the stitches, one of his favorite textures.

As expected, he worked up a sweat. The weight of his pack pressed the jacket, his sweater tunic, and his silk undertunic into a damp wad against his back. He didn't really care. The flex and surge of his legs muscles, the swing of his arms, felt good. Better to be out and active and sweaty than quiet and clean sitting by the hearth. He served as the trapunto specialist – *duoja*-imbued trapunto – for Rakas-lodge, so he did a lot of it. But he often worked out of doors. The light was better, and he didn't mind the cold. Embraced it, truly.

Around noon, the sun broke through the overcast in places, strengthening the golden highlights on the landscape around him, banishing the cool gray hues. The road turned toward the northwest and a fishery located there. Ivvar was headed southwest, so he took the trappers' trail running in the correct direction. It wound around dense thickets more tightly, but the terrain remained equally flat. A logging wain couldn't negotiate the narrower way with its sharp curves, but they presented no difficulty to a man on foot. Ivvar felt more intimately a part of the woods, reaching out to pat the tree trunks sometimes as he passed.

A short way along the trail he stopped at a free flowing stream. Patches of ice skimmed its shady edges, but the center ran clear. Ivvar found a spot in the lea of a holly thicket without snow and shed his pack, his jacket, and his snowshoes.

He made a quick meal of salmon jerky and dried apple strips. The savory taste of the jerky contrasted nicely with the sweetness of the apple. The cold, cold water in his canteen slipped down his throat deliciously, cooling him. He refilled it at the stream, noticing the abundant tracks of beaver and marten on the snowy banks. The trappers should have a good harvest, once they started working.

As he clipped his canteen back onto his belt, a breeze picked up, stronger than any movement of air through all the still morning. Far, far in the distance and very faint, a moaning roar sounded. The ice on the river breaking? A massive pine falling, its roots giving up the struggle reluctantly? He couldn't quite place it.

After restrapping his pack, he tied his snowshoes on, adjusting the leather thongs a little tighter – they'd stretched just a touch under the morning's use. Then he donned his jacket, hoisted his pack straps over his shoulders, and set off.

The overcast closed and thickened, returning the golden-white snow to cold white and chilling the air. Better for heated exertion, honestly. A few snowflakes floated down. The dark boles of the trees, vertical and somber, seemed suddenly ominous.

Ivvar lifted his chin and stepped up his pace, forgetting that he didn't want to catch up to Paiam. Forgetting that she was presumably somewhere ahead.

The snowfall thickened, but the air stayed still. The flakes formed a living curtain of motion, blanketing the pine branches high overhead, streaming down in scattered clearings between the trees. Ivvar paused to swap out his jacket for his wolf cloak. He wasn't cold, but the snout of the hood kept the snow out of his eyes. He noted fox tracks while he paused, as well as rabbit and possum. Why were they all headed south? That seemed a bit strange.

Later, wolf tracks crossed the trail, also pointing south.

Ivvar stopped. Frowning, he bent to examine the prints in the snow. Two wolves, likely a male and a female, moving fast. And southward. He sniffed: cold and fresh and clean, just as snow should smell.

The second breeze of the day arrived, from the northeast, blowing the snowfall at a gentle angle.

Then came that tortured roaring noise. Was it louder?

Ivvar's frown deepened.

He needed to get to some vantage from which to see across distance. And he'd travelled this way often enough, every four or five years, to know where he could get it. The land was largely flat, but mounded up into a lone hill or escarpment occasionally. There should be a bluff just a little out of his way.

He started looking for a large boulder with a flat top segmented by cracks into three pieces. The ice that had once pressed all this region flat thousands of years ago had left plenty of rocks behind. There was his landmark.

He departed the trail, threading through the trees to the north. The land lifted slightly as he went on, steepening and then ending abruptly in a short precipice with rockfall below it. This was one of the larger boulders brought by glaciers. Ivvar looked out across the treetops, dark needles showing in patches beneath the quilt of snow, all the way to the horizon, he knew. Except he couldn't see the horizon. He'd achieved the vantage he wanted, but the thickening snowflakes shut down the view to a few hundred paces.

The distant roaring sounded once again, so faint he could barely discern it. How loud must it be at its source to carry through the muffling of the snow? From what infernal throat did it issue? And why was he imagining some supernal creature? No ice tiger or north-bear could generate a roar like that! It must spring from the earth, or the earth's waters, to carry such power.

Ivvar shook his head. The ends of his dreadlocks flicked his shoulders. There was something . . . but he just couldn't quite bring it to mind. That was the problem with old age. Ill health and infirmity could be warded off with proper exertion and healthful eating. But the mind grew ever more full with experience and knowledge. Dredging up one mote of obscure information from the morass could be impossible.

He snorted and retraced his steps.

As the afternoon wore on, he began to think about where he would make camp for the night. There was a trappers' hut he'd used on previous trips, but on those trips he'd made his usual early start. He'd be bivouacking this evening. Probably in a clearing in the lea of another big boulder, the one the trappers called Tiger Crouching because of the way one side of it resembled the head and paws of that predator. It wasn't as massive as the bluff he'd sought earlier, but it made a nice shelter from any wind for a tent. And a stream ran through one side of the clearing there.

Ivvar quickened his pace yet again. The falling snow meant dark would descend sooner than on a clear day. And . . . he *did* like moving fast. A grin stretched his lips.

Half a league before his chosen campsite, a large stream crossed the trail. Ice still bound its edges, but the center showed dark water flowing fast and clear. Ivvar removed his snowshoes and clipped them to an outside ring on his pack. He'd need the gripping ability of his boiled wool boots in order to cross via the stepping stones placed by the trappers. The rocks were flat and steady, but slippery as an eel's skin from the falling snow.

He measured his steps carefully, placed his feet with even more care, and didn't skip the stones that he'd normally deem too close together.

He reached the other side safe and dry. Someone else ahead of him had been less fortunate. Broken ice and a broad swathe of mud showed where a fellow traveler had dragged him- or herself out of the water after falling. Paiam? Surely not. She had a reputation as canny as his; so much so that rumor of it reached his ears even though his grandchildren never spoke of her to him. Paiam wouldn't be falling into a brook in winter.

Despite this reassurance, he tied his snowshoe thongs quickly, and quickened his stride yet again.

Paiam relaxed her posture to lean back against the solid, peeled and squared logs behind her. This was the sauna, after all, a place meant for serenity and contemplation. And she felt serene. But she'd never favored slumping.

A smile curved her mouth. No, she preferred to meet life head on and always had, sometimes to her own detriment.

But here even she would soften.

The mellow gold of the old pine walls and benches invited it, as did the fierce heat licking her bare, tan-hued skin and the faint fresh scent of birch bark on the air, mingling with the tangier odor of cedar.

She exhaled, lifting the crown of her head slightly, pressing down through her feet onto the slats of the lower bench where they rested.

She'd chosen the upper bench, seeking the extra heat there. There was a reason she lolled in the sauna mid-morning, rough toweling under her, instead of tramping the snowy trail toward her destination. The heat would drive off the incipient cold she'd felt tickling her throat and nose when she first woke before dawn.

The tactic had worked too.

That hint of foulness at the back of her mouth – mucous gathering – was gone, as was the catch in her swallow and congestion in her nose.

She'd failed her planned early start, but her cold was on its way out without ever truly arriving. Well worth the delay. She'd need to leave soon, however, if she were going to leave today.

Was it time to sprinkle the hot stones with water for a last cleansing burst of steam? She had the sauna to herself, so she needn't consult the wishes of others.

No, not yet.

She'd bake in the dry heat a little longer, drive any vestiges of illness from her bones before she stirred.

Admit it, old woman, she admonished herself, *you're just indulging yourself.*

Perhaps she was, but it was a much younger Paiam who'd resisted indulgence and luxury.

I've not been that Paiam for many a decade now.

She surveyed her lanky body, naked as it was in this sacred space. Sacred to Hammarleedings anyway. She wasn't sure lowlanders felt the same.

The boniness of her frame struck her as it always did: knobby elbows and knees, the white line of the scar on the tan skin of her right thigh; the straightness of her narrow hips. At least she was strong. Old skin always sagged. The same for old breasts, no matter how small, and even nursing her daughter – all those decades ago – hadn't plumped up her bust line. But the strength in her calves and buttocks and belly gave firmness to her shape.

She might have claimed to be past vanity. She was certainly of an age to be past it, in her eighties. But in truth she was glad to be lean and fit, relieved that her breasts didn't hang to her waist, nor her belly round like a ripe pear. Plenty of her clan-sisters in Kaunis-lodge complained of just those characteristics.

So I'm vain.

But it was her own fitness that she valued most. Without strength, she wouldn't be here at The Mink and Mug, en route to the frontier lands of western Silmaren where the Reindeer People roamed. Without strength, she wouldn't be able to visit the new great grandbaby just born to her granddaughter Livli.

No, vanity was far from her worst sin.

Stubbornness. Temper. Rigidity. Those had delivered far worse consequences in her youth, and she'd beaten them back or – more truly – relinquished them. Some. Enough anyway. Her lips curved again. *I'm not perfect.* But who was?

Silly question. Regardless of how she compared to the ideal, it was her duty to work on her faults.

Except duty was another thing that hadn't served her well. She believed in cultivating strength, pruning weakness, but not for duty. For life. For joy. For freedom.

Yes, all those.

But "should" and "ought to" and duty didn't work. Not for her. She refused to live her life that way, even if the word did creep into her thoughts now and again.

Habit. Old habit.

She shifted on her sit bones, tugged the toweling under her straight. It had developed an uncomfortable wrinkle.

Now was the time for some steam.

She scooted down to the lower bench and bent for the dipper propped within the full cedar bucket on the floor slats. Just one ladle full, not more. A sauna wouldn't feel complete without the final burst of steam, but she craved the dry heat, not the moist.

With a quick gesture, she tossed the water onto the river rocks cradled within the open top compartment of the heater. The bottom compartment – the firebox – was vented and fed from the outside, a much safer option than the inside access present in some older saunas. The Mink and Mug was a classy establishment, despite the rugged frontiersmen who frequented it.

The water hit the hot rocks with a sharp hiss, and steam billowed into the air. The heat increased abruptly. Sweat broke out on Paiam's face. She was glad to be perched on the lower bench. The upper one would be even hotter.

Fire drives out ice.

How had she managed to be both fiery and icy in her young days? Somehow she had.

And now?

Still passionate, yes. But her fire had mellowed. And her ice . . . melted.

I like who I am now better.

Not everyone did. The rules-followers – and Kaunis still possessed its coterie of them – had liked the icier Paiam better.

But Ivvar would have liked this mellower Paiam she'd become.

Now where had that thought come from? She hadn't considered her linking-brother – what lowlanders named as husband – in oh-so-long. Why now?

But, yes, Ivvar would have enjoyed her progress from rule-bound to . . . what was she now? A rule-breaker?

Not exactly.

Ivvar was a rule-breaker.

She still remembered his most shocking breach of tradition. It had been after the spring herd-luring sixty odd years ago. She'd summoned the wild sheep with her *duoja*, calling them from the high mountain crags for their shearing, as her people did, and presiding with the holy caller over the rituals of the day. She'd be missing this spring's herd-luring. Biret, plump kind Biret, would fill her place, guiding the beasts down to the waiting hands of the Tukeva-brothers and their skillful shears.

Paiam missed it already, even though the day for it was yet three eight-days hence. Missed the bracing mountain breeze and the clean-swept sky. Missed the unruly and rambunctious consciousness of the sheep, sensed through her probing *duoja*, a mystical shepherd's crook. Missed the beauty of the seeking *duoja* itself, swirling in graceful spirals of air, playing a poignant music unheard by the ear, but perceived by the mind. Missed the shock of first contact with the sheep, when they bent to her will and came bleating to the sloping meadow above her home lodge, with its damp green turf and the gathered crowd of Hammarleedings, the men chanting low and the women keening high while they stamped in a dance that lasted from sunup to sundown.

Sixty-some years ago, when Hilka had been the lead lurer and Paiam the subsidiary one, Ivvar had embraced her when the last shorn sheep bucked away across the meadow toward the heights and freedom.

"Come with me, Paiam!" he'd urged. "We'll pitch my tent beside Peili Tarn and watch the stars light the sky in its still water. Then we'll link all night long."

His face glowed, radiant in his love for her, eyes beaming down into hers, into the heart of her.

She'd drawn back from him, appalled that he'd propose such an escapade. Hammarleeding men and women linked – enjoyed sex as she supposed the lowlanders would say – only within the elaborate ceremonies that were part of the high fete days. Casual linking at the couple's own desire just wasn't done.

She'd given in, gone with him, and rued it ever after. That was when their daughter Sarvet had been conceived, on that magical, ecstatic night of joy. Unsanctioned. Forbidden. Exquisite.

She could still feel the intensity of their joining.

She'd wanted him. Wanted him too much.

At least, that's what she'd thought at the time. Now, many decades later, she wasn't so sure. She'd been right, but she'd also been wrong. It wasn't her love for Ivvar, or his for her, that had been the problem. But she'd thought it was. Thought she'd sinned by loving Ivvar more than the goddess Sias, giver of gifts. Thought she'd trespassed by longing for Ivvar's touch more than she'd longed for Sias' blessing. Sias and her legendary champion Duoja.

Certainly trouble had come of it. Her daughter suffered a birth injury when she exited Paiam's womb nine months later, and Paiam and Ivvar had fought far more than they'd loved on the fete days when the Tukeva-bothers visited the Kaunis-sisters.

Paiam had ended their linking – their marriage – when little Sarvet turned three. Ivvar had ended more than that when Sarvet turned five. He forsook Tukeva-lodge forever, claiming Rakas-lodge for his home.

It was better so.

They'd hurt one another too much.

She could still see his face on their last parting, eyes grave. He'd found peace in his decision and, eventually, so had she. Though she carried her guilt even now. Muted, almost forgotten, but present nonetheless. In her own judging, her wrongs outweighed his. He'd been wise for both of them.

And, in time, she'd recognized his wisdom. When Sanay was born – their first great grandchild to arrive in the camps of the Reindeer People – she'd arranged her itinerary to be sure she didn't encounter Ivvar when she traveled to meet the baby. The same for the next Reindeer great grandchild.

But not this one. Why hadn't she made sure Ivvar bided at his home in Rakas-lodge?

It shouldn't matter. He always waited until the infant grew older to make his trip. Paiam suspected he liked the games one could play with a toddler better than the simple cradling a newborn required.

She sighed. Sometimes she still wished she could tell Ivvar, "I'm sorry."

But not today. Today she was headed yet farther away from the Fiordhammars that were the Hammarleeding home, and she'd remain so for half the year. When she returned in late summer, perhaps she'd revisit the issue.

The steam of the sauna had dissipated, her skin dried, and the scorching heat abated to a solid comfort in her bones. She felt cleansed.

Now to gather a few last sundries and depart The Mink and Mug.

It took surprisingly little time. She'd already packed her gear and arranged for Maitresse Odissa to store her skis. Well before noon, Paiam followed the road west, tramping forward on snowshoes with a smooth, loose stride through lightly falling scintillas of ice. When she reached the trail turn-off, the snowfall thickened, the flakes growing large like morsels of clotted cream, but there was no wind. Just the living curtain of frozen crystals, the black branchless trunks of the pines going up and up to their tufted tops against a cloud-banked sky – and her, alone in the late winter woods.

She wondered if she'd hear again the strange music – *duoja* music – that had teased her during the last eight-day before she'd arrived at The Mink and Mug. Lowlander magic – keyholding – worked quite differently than Hammarleeding magic. What was the source of those half-heard notes, so similar to *duoja*, but not quite?

She'd remain alert. Which was wise in the wilderlands, even if you weren't tracking a mystery.

Behind the crunch of the snow under her steps, the creak of the leather webbing of her snowshoes, and the click of their ashwood frames – as the inner edge of her stepping foot slid over the inner edge of her planted foot – lay the deep silence of the backcountry and the special soft muffling silence of the spilling snow. Silence and the resinous scent of the pines, their sap beginning to move as spring approached.

She relished it.

Her knees and ankles felt warm and loose, despite how stiff and sore she'd awoken. The sauna had taken care of that of course, but she'd been neglecting her morning stretches – the dawn branching sequence, as the holy caller back home named it – on this long journey into Silmaren's western frontier to visit her new great-grandbaby. The exertion of snowshoeing would keep her leg muscles pliable, but she could feel the slight catch that plagued her right shoulder as she swung her balancing poles. Better not skip the dusk branching sequence this evening or her old joints would only protest louder tomorrow.

But – ah! – this was glorious! Lovely flat terrain, so much easier to traverse than the steep slopes of her home mountains. And a beautifully firm snow trail – packed down by the trappers, winding around the rough-barked tree boles and into the breathing veil of snowfall.

She paused beside one of the straight trunks, listening.

No, nothing.

She tipped her face up, welcoming the feathery caress of the snowflakes against her chilled nose and cheeks. They were the only parts of her that were cold. The thick boiled wool of her knee-high boots meant her toes never suffered the nip of winter, even amidst weather far more bitter than this. The ecru wool of her leggings and tunic over her thistlesilk undergarments warmed the rest of her. Likewise her thistlesilk gloves and goatskin over-mittens. While her sheepskin cape with her unusual hood kept her dry.

She still got strange looks from the lowlanders for her hood. Even now, when so many more of her mountain people visited the valleys. Her grandsons sported head gear of ram, ice leopard, and fox. Hers was a ewe. The creature's upper skull created a stiff extension that protected her face from rain and snow, while its fleeces padded the bone both inside and out. The attached cape turned its brown suede-side to the elements, the fuzzy fleeces, in.

It was a practical design, but the lowlanders still stared.

Of course, the glass eyes that gave the animal hood a semblance of life might have something to do with that!

Paiam chuckled and pushed the front flap of her cape aside to get at her leather water sack. The cork stopper came easily out of the horn nozzle. She lifted the bag, strap still in place over her shoulder – the left one – and tipped.

A clear stream of water arced out and onto her tongue. Ah, cold and liquid and refreshing, all the way down her throat. But a touch peaty and flat, without the mineral briskness of the spring at home.

She re-corked the nozzle, re-settled the vessel at her hip, and drew her cape closed across her front. About to step forward, she hesitated, listening again.

Where . . . where . . . ?

Ah! There! Ahead of her.

A silver arpeggio of notes, not quite a flute, not quite a constellation of chimes, quick and lilting – beautiful. Yet not hanging in the snow-flocked air. No, playing in some inaccessible ether, heard not with the ear, but with the magical arts of *duoja*.

She strode out more quickly, swinging her trekking poles briskly, eager to find the source of this strange phenomenon. The snow was sticking to the trail now, covering the firmer surface created by the trappers coming in from the wilds, but not thick enough to slow her.

Her way passed out from the intimacy of the pine forest, many pillared with its tall straight trunks, and into a spruce glade, more open to the sky and clouds and snow because of the broad bases and dwindling tops of the firs. A sudden gust of wind drove the snow against her face, cold and stinging pinpricks on her cheeks. The silence carried the wider, crisper quality of large spaces: meadows and mountainsides.

Another sprinkle of singing chimes called to her. She quickened her pace. Was she nearing whatever it was that played?

The trail re-entered the pines, quieting the silence to a more muffled essence, the hush of a yarn closet or a linen store. The snow carpeting the trail acquired a rumpled look. Was someone ahead of her? An early logger? Unlikely. The nearest mill lay to the northwest, not in the southwest where this track headed. An animal? Bold fox or incautious hare? Just as unlikely. Most beasts avoided the haunts of men.

But something traveled the trail ahead of her. A good hour ahead. She knew the look of fresh, newly formed prints in snow. And she knew the look of old, blunted prints largely filled-in by continuing snowfall. These were the latter.

Something scuffed out ahead. Something. Perhaps the originator of those magical chimes.

They sounded again: a silver and gold staccato with a mellow, resinous undertone, drawn out to a long-fading murmur.

She *was* getting closer.

But she remained just as baffled about who or what it was. Her own herd-luring *duoja* sounded like wind in the trees or breezes across a lake, not music. Her granddaughter's healing *duoja* brought to mind the babble of brook water over stones or the rush of a waterfall plunging beyond its brink. Or, sometimes, ocean breakers against a rocky beach.

This music – it was *duoja*, but it wasn't anything she'd encountered before. She followed it, winding through the forest, noting that the footprints grew more definite, eventually definite enough to relinquish their mystery. Someone on long thin snowshoes went before her, someone with a long, long stride.

Whoever it was turned aside from the trail twice, going some distance out and then returning to travel onward. Now why? What might stir his curiosity? Did he too hear the strange music? Or did he cause it? She was increasingly sure he was a man. His stride was longer than hers, and she was tall.

The snowfall slackened, then ceased altogether. Occasionally a branch dumped its load of snow. The still air stirred and carried a drift of the powder through the trees.

Paiam paused at the crossing of the Skummende, one of the larger streams en route to the ambit of the Minmahal, the tribe of Reindeer People with whom Livli roamed.

It seemed there were *two* travelers ahead of her. One the tall, long-striding man. The other . . . someone in trouble.

The man had removed his snowshoes to traverse the water. The trail approached the Skummende directly through a shallow defile in the earth. Eight flat stepping stones, surrounded by a dark and swirling current, led from snowy bank to snowy bank. The man's footprints stood out clearly, crisply denting the snow. Paiam studied them. Something about them caught her attention. Why was that?

Her attention shifted to the other markings. Someone in a hurry. Someone small and light. Someone who had fallen, just short of the far bank, dragging herself out of the frigid water and across the shattered ice along the edge, then up the steeper trail there. Someone who was likely now dead of exposure. Unless the longstrider had caught up with her in time.

Or unless she possessed a special magic – one that spread sparkling music on the air? – that could warm her before she froze.

Paiam compressed her lips and bent to loosen the thongs binding her snowshoes. She looped them to a ring on the side of her pack.

The cloud cover thinned, and despite the drawing on of the afternoon, the daylight strengthened and acquired a warmer hue.

She surveyed the abruptly welcoming woodlands. *There*. That would do: a new-grown sapling, barely half a palm in girth. She propped her trekking poles against the trunk of a larger tree. They were good for balancing as she walked, light and whippy. But she wanted something sturdier for crossing the stream.

She slung her pack down and drew her knife from the scabbard secured to its other side.

Sap already flowed through the trunk of the sapling, but her knife was sharp, making short work of cutting through the fibrous wood near the roots. A few quick slashes removed the slender branches and her staff was ready. Retrieving her pack and poles, she moved surely onto the first stepping stone.

Yes, as she'd thought, the surface was slippery from the fast accumulating snow. Her woolen boots, the fibers sticky and flexible despite the thickness of the fabric composing the soles, helped her feet to grip the blanketed rock, but she was glad to grasp the sapling staff, its tip planted firmly in the streambed. *She* would not fall.

On the other side, she let her staff go, re-fastened her snowshoes, and took her trekking poles in either hand. What *was* it about Longstrider's footprints?

It was only as she set off again that she realized it. Divine Duoja! He was Hammarleeding!

Cassende was cold, oh-so-cold. Bone deep in her marrow. So cold she could not shiver. She could feel the snow around her, banked against her ribs. Her eyelids were stiff, holding her eyes closed. Did flakes still pour from the sky as though flowing from old Mother Holle's pitcher to fill the air like feathers in a pillow fight?

Her cheeks were too frozen to feel them, if it were so.

Even the throbbing of her bruises had receded.

Was it indeed mounds of snow that buried her? Or was it stones? The stones flung by scared villagers? Was she dying under a rough cairn of rock? Cold and heavy and pressing her down?

Or was it the snow? Snow ticking against stone as it fell down and down from the clouds?

She couldn't get her thoughts clear.

She'd purchased boots in a shop in Andham, redolent with oiled leathers and where they'd taken her for a sweet old lady. Later she'd realized that boots would not be enough for the chill of northern Silmaren in winter and sought something warmer in a tiny hamlet without a name. Or without one known to her. The craftsman had sold her mink-lined gaiters, glancing at her nervously all the while. She could still see his quick eyes darting away, his pink tongue touching his upper lip.

He'd known. Known what she was. Known she was dangerous.

Was it he who'd warned the others? Or were they just boys with more *nous* than most? And a yen to bully?

They'd thrown the stones hard, bruising her sides, her hips, her shoulders, her legs. A stone to her head might have killed her. Why had they not aimed higher?

She'd not been able to bring herself to retaliate. They were children. Too like her own Stefano and undeserving of . . . what she would deliver. There was the problem. She had no nuance with which to calibrate her response. It could be all and lethal. Or it could be nothing. There was no inbetween.

Did she lie under their flung stones? No, she'd escaped them and their malice, fled farther north still, just as she fled her home in Pavelle, the little rose-covered cottage outside Osier where she'd reared her children and loved her spouse.

It had all happened so quickly, there at home.

She'd believed herself safe, sheltered by the new protocol rolled out by the Minister of Incantors himself. The cure brought by his antiphonic healers had eased the worst symptoms of her dread disease, while the decrees of his heralds declared her protected, innocuous, and deserving of help.

The villagers hadn't believed it, of course. Now she knew that too well. But they'd obeyed; accepted the healers; refrained from persecution of the diseased ones.

And Cassende had improved, lost her wrinkles and her joint pain, regained her clear sight and clear thinking. Along with the others. The incredible hope brought from the capital was true. They would live normal, healthy lives again.

She and her husband had cried and embraced when they realized the full truth of her reprieve. She could still feel his firm cheek against hers, wet with tears. The sudden heave of his chest as he encircled her in his arms. "Dear Cass, dearest Cass," he'd muttered. "You'll see your grandchildren yet."

But for him, she'd have died when the villagers fired the retreat bungalow one afternoon while she'd been there for her regular antiphonic treatment.

He'd been waiting for her, reading a periodical no doubt, and seen the mob approaching. He'd hustled her out the back and home, then diverted their angry neighbors while she escaped north with only the coin purse he pressed upon her at the last moment.

If only she'd gone south to Bazinthiad, the source of the new leniency for her kind.

But her cottage lay north of Osier, and it seemed wise to leave the village behind as rapidly as possible. The farther north she went, the more hostile the people became. And it had never proved possible to circle back around to the south.

Had her darling Davide survived the torches of the troll-hunters? He'd pushed her away as he ran to meet them, and she'd gone, heartsore. How had their dream of happy, old age expired so rapidly? Killed by fear and ignorance, that was how.

And now, after his sacrifice, she too would perish, lost in the snows of the far north.

She could smell the freshness of the pure air, taste the cold ice of winter.

Here she would lie, frozen until spring, when the melt would rot her bones.

A ghost of warmth brushed her closed eyelids, stole across her chilled cheek. Here was the illusion of heat that signaled the end, when her body mistook its sinking lassitude for life returning.

Ivvar shook his head.

Someone was in trouble. Really serious trouble.

Sodden, staggering tracks in the snow led away from the stream bank along the trail. Whoever had fallen in the water, breaking through the cracked ice at its edge, hadn't stopped to dry off or warm up. She – Ivvar was nearly certain she was a she, her footprints too small to be a man's – had merely picked herself up and pressed onward.

Poor choice. Deadly choice.

The snowfall was slackening, but the cold would penetrate rapidly through soaked garments. Penetrate and kill.

Ivvar was almost running; arms pumping and snowshoes creaking under his thunderous strides.

He felt the sweat break out afresh on his back.

The uneven tracks of his quarry merged into a curving skid punctuated by a lumpy hollow pressed into the snow at the base of a tree trunk.

She'd slipped and fallen. Then picked herself up again, for the irregular tracks continued past the evidence of her tumble.

Duoja's demons! Did she imagine she could run herself warm and dry?

Three skids and two falls later – the woman's, not his own – Ivvar burst into the clearing where he'd planned to camp. Tall columns of pines clustered to his left, while a glade of spruce curved away to his right, climbing the incline there that ended in an abrupt drop-off: the Crouching Tiger.

The snowfall stopped altogether, leaving the faintest icy powder in the air.

Ivvar followed the trail alongside the rising ground, ignoring the likeness of the bluff above him to its name – Tiger – all his concentration on his chase and the increasingly erratic steps he followed.

Abruptly, he flung away from the trapper trail, diving into the small, white meadow pooling around the foot of the rock face.

A dark huddle of wool blotted the snow below the Tiger's jowl.

Ivvar checked his furious pace, approaching with a measured gait.

She'd landed on her back, and the hood of her coat – deep blue, he could see now that he stood over her, despite the ice crusting its wet surface – had fallen away.

Her hair was silver and coiled in two buns over each ear. The firmness of her skin belied the age implied by her hair. He suspected she would show roses in her cheeks were she not dying. But she was old. He could see it in the hunch of her back and shoulders, the frailty of her wrists and neck, the pucker of her closed eyelids. Frail and pale and . . . dead?

Rapidly he detached his snowshoes to kneel beside her. Did she yet breathe? He bent to her face, felt a puff of warmth against his cheek. She lived!

What was it about her that gave him pause?

He studied her a moment more.

Hunched spine within her sodden coat. Ears hidden by her coiled hair. A strange elongation of her tilted nose.

Demons! She was a troll-witch!

That explained a lot. Why an old woman roamed the winter woods. Why she was alone. Why she ran away from help.

Her kind were hunted in civilized lands. Hunted and killed before their magic – the dreaded *incantatio*, that both made them powerful and drove them insane – erupted in a lethal explosion that destroyed a village or made all its inhabitants ill.

Trolls were dangerous vermin, no question. Village destroyers? Ivvar wasn't so sure. But he'd seen one break his grandson's leg. And heard the story of how another tried to roast a lowlander boy for his Yuletide feast.

It was his duty to kill this troll, just in case her magic allowed her to survive her dunking. Silmarish law demanded it. His own prudence counseled it. And yet . . . he couldn't do it.

She reminded him of his *maghra* – his grandmother – dainty and sweet. How she'd regaled him with succulent hoolinberries when he visited Kaunis-lodge as a lad and told him tale after tale of pegasi and gryphons and ice wyrms beside the warm tile stove in her parlor.

Shaking his head, he slid his pack straps off his shoulders, lowered it to the ground, and dragged his ground cloth from an outer pouch. Unfolding the oiled canvas just enough to accommodate the troll-witch, he spread it next to her, then gently lifted her in his arms.

She lay there so lightly, like a bird or a kitten.

Her heavy coat would have to come off. She needed to be warm and dry, and the blanket-like wool would never give up its moisture in time.

He worked at the buttons one-handed, struggling with their recalcitrance, then tugging at one sleeve. The second sleeve was easier.

Under her coat – a lowlander coat – she wore the southern garb of a Giralliyan: quilted silk surcoat, silk tabard beneath that, and a long tunic with a chemise peeking out at the neck, all in shades of rich blue.

So she'd come farther than he thought. Not a Silmarish lowlander fleeing her hamlet – or her city –

to hide in the wilds, but a citizen of the Giralliyan empire fleeing that sophisticated land for rustic safety.

Ivvar frowned.

He'd heard they treated trolls differently in the south. That they'd discovered a cure for the disease that made them what they were.

Why had she fled? Did she prefer to keep her magical powers, despite their cruel price of ostracism, insanity, and death? Would she awake spitting acrid orange light – the mark of *incantatio* – if he saved her?

Ivvar laid her down on the groundcloth, then rummaged in his pack for his sewing kit. He pricked his finger getting a needle out of the needle case. It was already threaded in blue.

Settling into a cross-legged position beside the troll-witch, he held one edge of her surcoat placket and began to sew: three decorative knots, a satin-stitched teardrop, three decorative knots, a twining vine curve. With each prod of the needle, he pushed his *duoja* along the thread: the warmth of flame, the warmth of love, the warmth of blood itself.

A bubble of warm air coalesced around his fingers, expanded to surround his hands, expanded yet again to envelop his body and that of the troll-witch.

A few snowflakes fell from the high overcast, but

they turned to tepid raindrops when they encountered the heated sphere.

Ivvar sewed.

The daylight acquired a golden hue as the afternoon closed down.

Ivvar sewed, leaving a tracery of tone-on-tone spirals in his needle's wake, from the neck of the surcoat to its ankle-hem.

He knotted his thread and laid aside his needle, but did not stop the flow of his *duoja*. Fully absorbed in an inner rhythm, he extracted his quilting wand and stabbed the empty air, stitching his pattern of warmth into its essence. Warm sun, warm blankets, warm summer.

The troll-witch opened her eyes. They were blue, and her whole face came alive with them.

"Thank you," she breathed.

As Paiam strode forward, the thin overcast still hid the sky, but the sun found a break in the clouds near the horizon. The long, low rays of late afternoon flooded the forest, striping the snowy ground with the dark shadows of tree trunks and striking bright scintillas from icicles dripping from the high pine branches.

Paiam focused her attention on the footprints she followed: the stumbling ones of the first traveler who'd fallen in the stream and the running ones of the Hammarleeding man who evidently hoped to rescue the unfortunate person ahead of him.

What *was* it about those Hammarleeding tracks?

If she were a hunter of the *onderneming*, like her old linking brother, she'd know. But she'd never learned the subtleties of reading the wood signs left by passersby, just the obvious basics that any woman of the mountains should possess.

Another ripple of the otherworldly music that had played increasingly during this day's trek swelled, a fast chiming of bells, fluid and sweet, a celebration of the advent of all good things. She could sense a crescendo approaching, the harbinger of something new on its way. Would she get there in time? Would she see what was coming, what instrument emanated these divine harmonies, who the player was?

Or would the hymn cease before she arrived at the source to witness it?

Paiam slowed, trying to unravel the puzzles teasing her: the first footprints, the second footprints, and the unearthly song. Even the bands of sunlight and shadow flickering across her face as she moved forward seemed to form a part of some intense whole.

The two sets of footprints belonged to one story, clearly. The sunlit woods and the music seemed unrelated. Why did they feel related to her?

Then came the hint of a lower resonance, as of a bow drawn over the strings of a bass viol, but far, far away. A new entrant to the chorale.

That faint drawn-out note increased Paiam's sense of a riddle confronting her. There was something she should know. Something she should figure the answer to. Something . . . familiar?

The deep tones anchoring the rippling melodic ones grew rapidly more audible – nearer – as she progressed. Sonorous and reverberant, felt in her bones, but like the chiming melody not heard by the ear: *duoja*. But unlike those chimes, this *was* the magic of the Hammarleedings: a spinner spinning strength into her thread, a brewer brewing health into her mead, a weaver weaving comfort into her cloth.

Abruptly Paiam speeded her stride and burst into the clearing surrounding the Tiger Rock.

A spinner, a brewer, a weaver. Or a quilter quilting warmth into a coat?

Paiam rounded the Rock to see her former linking-brother seated before a bundle in the snow and performing trapunto on the air.

Ivvar. Of course! Ivvar.

The long stride, the chivalrous intent, the low-toned *duoja* with its familiar rhythm. It could only be Ivvar, no doubt traveling toward their new great grandchild, just as was she.

Paiam shook her head, marveling at both her surprise and her lack of it, the two opposite sentiments bizarrely commingled in her breast.

Ivvar.

But who was this he'd found and succored?

An old woman? She had white hair, but . . . she looked young.

An old Giralliyan woman? Paiam recognized the style of those garments, but . . . why would a Giralliyan travel so far north in Silmaren?

An ailing old woman? The faint flush in her cheeks proved that Ivvar's *duoja* had restored her from the cold, but her eyes bore a strange slant and her nose . . .

"Duoja in her demesne! Ivvar, she's dangerous!" Paiam's voice emerged as a harsh croak, dry from her silence all the afternoon. "She's a troll!"

"I know."

He'd neither flinched nor stiffened. Not when she spoke. Not when she'd approached so close behind his back. But he'd have been aware of her, just as she'd sensed him, at some distance. Not as the notes or sounds that Paiam perceived, however. Ivvar had always claimed he discerned *duoja* as ranges of hot and cold or, sometimes, as pressure. Had he felt her as a chill breeze approaching or a gust of strong wind? No doubt she felt as strangely familiar through his *duoja* sense as he did to her. Had he expected her? He seemed utterly unsurprised.

He continued his *duoja* stitching of the air, feeding the bubble of warmth he'd created, maintaining it against the late winter chill. The troll, eyes open, but silent, watched his moving hands.

"Have you spare garments, Paiam? Cassende is warm enough, but her robes remain damp. I need dry things for her to change into."

"Ivvar, are you mad? What were you thinking! A troll?"

His stitching never ceased. "I suspect you know." His tone was dry.

Yes, she knew. Knew his warm heart. Knew his charity. But . . a troll-witch!

Paiam sighed and slung her pack to the ground. At least the witch was doing little right now, perhaps drained by her ordeal, temporarily dispossessed of her power to wield the deadly *incantatio* of trolls. Biding her time?

Oh, this was *not* practical! Drat the man and his kindness! A troll!

Paiam repressed a second sigh. Pulled out her spare undertunic and trews, a gray sweater tunic and leggings, thick short-hose.

"I suppose you want me to dress her." The words came out more acerbically than she intended.

Ivvar glanced over his shoulder, smiling. Paiam felt the tightness easing in her breastbone. He'd always been able to calm her, even when she was most riled, when she was young. Not enough to save their linking, but sufficient to soothe an argument. She felt her lips smiling back at him.

"Let's see what Cassende can manage on her own, shall we?"

Cassende, huh? So the witch had a name. Paiam had encountered a troll-witch only once before, long, long ago when she was a little girl. She could still remember the old woman's maddened eyes, her sallow and drooping skin, her rotted breath. That witch had screamed nonsensical words with no meaning, and an acrid orange light crackled from her toward Paiam. Paiam had felt her heart stop in her chest. She'd fallen, unable to breath. And then breathed again when her grandmother slapped her chest. The men had killed the troll while Paiam lay gasping.

That witch had no name.

This one . . .

Ivvar's voice murmured, "Cassende, try to sit."

The troll stirred, heaved, but didn't make it upright. Her eyes darted from Ivvar to Paiam.

"Paiam, will you help her?"

There was nothing Paiam felt less like doing.

Kneeling down in the snow, she supported Cassende's shoulders. Her own shoulder twinged. Ivvar's hands stitched warmth into the air.

"I beg your pardon, frualte," the troll gasped. So Cassende spoke the Hamish tongue of the Silmarish lowlanders. Most Giralliyans living along the northern coast of the continent did. And she was cultured, judging by her use of "frualte." But Paiam didn't care to be called "high lady." Nor to use the term. The Hammarleedings had been largely unaffected by the brief rule of the conquering Hathorlynd nobility over Silmaren a generation ago, but many lowlanders retained considerable resentment for anything smacking of aristocracy. Paiam shared their views.

"Can you clothe yourself, maitresse?"

Cassende nodded, but her struggle to remove her surcoat ended with nothing accomplished, her frail arms falling to her lap.

Paiam took one edge of the troll's surcoat between her fingers. Newly embroidered by Ivvar's stitching by the looks of it. Apparently he'd begun on the silk and only switched to air further into his rescue. Stitching air was harder than stitching cloth. Paiam eased the garment over Cassende's shoulders, then pulled it out from under her. The troll winced as the surcoat came away. Was she bruised from her fall?

Cassende's tabard was of the style open down both sides and lifted easily over her head. The tunic, with long sleeves and no opening save the neck was harder. Paiam scrunched it up under Cassende's hips. The troll flinched again, but raised her arms – just barely – so Paiam could pull the whole thing up and off.

The sleeveless chemise, rucked up to the troll's knees, revealed dark purple blotches on Cassende's pale limbs.

Paiam hissed, moved to compassion in spite of herself. "Who did this to you?"

Cassende shivered, goose bumps pricking out on her mottled skin. She glanced at Paiam, then back at her own lap. "Scared villagers, frualte." Her voice was low and sad. "They've been taught that trolls are perilous. And many are. How should they know – or act – differently?"

Paiam bit her lip. The troll seemed almost civilized. Sane. Moderate. Coherent. How was such a thing possible? Wielding *incantatio* – troll-magic – damaged the user beyond repair. Paiam had felt the dangerous rage of a troll-witch in the heart of her body. She knew in her sinews that trolls required extermination.

But Cassende inspired her pity.

Paiam handed her the undertrews. Likely she'd feel more comfortable pulling them on before they removed the clammy chemise.

Cassende hunched forward, drawing up her knobby knees, then stopped.

Ah! The boots would need to go. They were stout leather with long laces and stiff, thick leather soles. No wonder Cassende had slipped on the stepping stones. Lowlander footgear gave so little traction. And the fur gaiters around her ankles, while helpful in conserving warmth, would do nothing toward gripping rock. Cassende would have done better to have exchanged her Giralliyan sandals for Hammarleeding boots.

Paiam leaned in to pick at the laces. The wet knots refused to come undone. She jerked her knife from its scabbard, noting the troll's hiss of alarm only after the first knot parted beneath the honed edge. "These must come off, maitresse," she reassured her.

Cassende managed to pull the trews on and her chemise off. After that the clothing change went faster. Once the witch sat bundled in Paiam's bed roll with Paiam's clothes on her body and Paiam's short-hose on her feet, Ivvar's arms fell to his sides.

The deep resonance of his *duoja* ceased.

Only the higher notes of the racing bell melody – the one Paiam had been hearing intermittently for the past eight days – continued. Its rhythm was faster, the unknown and unseen creator frenetically busy.

Ivvar looked quietly at Paiam.

Paiam looked uncomfortably at Ivvar.

What in the north did one say to one's former lover when the last time you'd set eyes on him was more than fifty years ago? When you'd blamed him for . . . too many things? When he'd left his brother-lodge forever especially so he wouldn't have to see you on fete days?

When you met him after all that long drink of time in the midst of helping a criminal foe?

Paiam just looked, saying nothing.

Ivvar smiled. That dear, slow smile that used to make her heart turn over. He had the same bony nose, lean cheeks, high cheek bones. The crow's feet at his eyes were deeper. He'd already possessed light ones from squinting while he chased the *onderneming* in his youth. The stubble on his square chin was silver now, not black; the wooly, shoulder-length ropes of his hair, gray and white. But the gold flecks in his gray-green eyes were the same.

"Dear Pai, do you mind?" Same deep, calm voice, but . . . did *she* mind? Surely he was the one to mind.

"I'll never mind again," she heard herself answering. Was she mad?

His eyes seemed fathoms deep. "Truly?"

She couldn't answer that. Not now, when the wrong words could move them both to wrong choices.

She exerted herself, seeking an inner coolness. "Now isn't the moment," she asserted, her voice dry. But a smile tugged at her lips, echoing his.

He laughed. "Cassende to tend, camp to make, strange noises on the air?"

That last item on his list startled her. Did he, too, hear the magical chimes still ringing in her *duoja*-sense? How could he, a touch practitioner? Abruptly her emotions fell aside.

"Ivvar, what plays those divine melodies? Do you know?"

The affection shining in his face gave way to puzzlement.

"Melodies? No, a roaring like no other I can call to mind. And yet I'd say I've heard it before."

Even as he spoke, his head lifted and he turned his gaze toward the trees.

"There! Did you catch it?"

No, she hadn't. What had he heard? Something other than what she did evidently.

"I heard it," came a faint voice.

Paiam's head swiveled back with Ivvar's to regard Cassende.

"Do you recognize it?" demanded Ivvar.

Cassende shook her head. "No, herralte."

"I'm Ivvar. Ivvar Dainar-spring, Cassende. And this is my friend Paiam Geira-spring."

Paiam held her left hand over her right before her chest and nodded in the polite form of greeting. It seemed no longer possible to view Cassende as anything but a woman deserving respect and courtesy. As crazy as that was. Not dangerous. Not criminal. Not vermin. On Ivvar's head be it.

"Balance be yours, Paiam Geira-spring." Cassende was rapidly regaining her own balance, evidently.

And Ivvar was regaining his.

"Paiam, I must check further into what sounds almost like an avalanche. It cannot be that in these flat lands, but I fear it is nothing benign." He was strapping his snowshoes back on as he spoke, closing and tying his pack. "Will you tend to Cassende while I am gone?"

He hoisted his pack up and paused, looking her straight in the eye.

Why did she feel that familiar mix of exasperation and affection? Except this time it made her happy, not annoyed.

"I'll take care of her."

A firm nod in response and he was gone. The sun sank below the tree tops, casting long stripes of gold and black across the snow-blanketed clearing. Paiam turned back to their charge.

"Maitresse, are you warm? And dry?"

There were other questions and to spare to ask the woman. Where was she from? Why was she here? What was she doing? But all of them could wait. Night was coming. The sun took a long time setting in these farthest northerly reaches, and the sky stayed bright a good long stretch after, but doing later what needed to be done now was never wise in the backcountry. Camp chores called.

Cassende tilted her head to one side. "I am warm, thanks be to Herr Dainar-spring, and I am dry, thanks be to you, frualte."

"Then I must set up camp before dark. Do you stay wrapped in those blankets while I go about it."

"Why do you help me, frualte?" Cassende's query was cool, almost detached – curious, not a challenge – her face calmly interested. "You'd prefer not to, wouldn't you?"

Indeed she'd prefer not to. Why hadn't she fought Ivvar harder on this? She didn't have an answer. For herself, or for Cassende. "We'll talk after." It came out more curtly than she'd meant it, but there was work to do.

Putting up her tent was a fiddly business of sliding bamboo pole sections into one another, poking the ends into the pockets at the corners, attaching the middles with innumerable ties, and pounding the stakes into the thawing ground below the snow. Fiddly, but she'd done it many a time, and could get through it quickly.

Once the tent was up and ready, well away from the trees, she glanced over at Cassende. She slumped, eyes closed, likely dozing after her ordeal. Paiam sniffed. She'd be well enough.

The cusp of the season was a good time for deadfall. Winter storms had shaken many a branch from its mooring and blown weak trees down. Paiam dragged several large logs out of the woods, and then switched to gathering kindling. When at last she built her fire and lit it, dusk had claimed the ground, although the sky remained bright.

She set a pan of snow to melt over the flames, and went to wake Cassende from her doze.

"Maitresse? Come sit nearer the fire."

Cassende blinked up at her, bewildered. Paiam offered her hand. After a moment, Cassende gripped it, attempted to rise, and fell back.

"Get your feet well under you," Paiam advised.

Cassende nodded and shifted. On her second attempt she made it. Paiam steadied her. The troll-woman's head came barely above Paiam's shoulder.

Seated before the fire, side by side on Ivvar's ground cloth, they sipped broth made from a bouillon pastille that Paiam crumbled into the hot water. She inhaled the steam, rich and savory with odors of the meat, then took a sip. *Mmm.* Not too hot, but warming all the way down. She glanced over at Cassende. The woman cupped her bowl between both hands, holding it below her chin, eyes closed. While Paiam watched, she took a long, long swallow, then sighed and opened her eyes.

"It's good," she said.

Paiam bit her lip. She was about to be rude and knew it. But old women were allowed to be rude. Or at least they could get away with it. And she needed to know more, a lot more, about Cassende.

"Are you seeking the court of a renegade troll-queen or troll-prince? Do you know of one forming on the tundra north of here?"

That was blunt. Too blunt.

Cassende's face, open from being tended, from the warmth, closed.

"No." Her voice was quiet, not resentful. "I know of no such, nor would I join one if there were."

"Then what are you doing here?" Paiam's own voice had sharpened. "If not to escape your death, to find shelter under a troll more powerful than yourself, why would you risk the backcountry so unprepared? Why else do trolls flee north?"

Cassende took another long swallow of her broth.

"You did not hear what Herralte Dainar-spring heard?"

"I did not." What did that have to do with Cassende's presence here?

"But you do hear something?"

Paiam narrowed her eyes. The *duoja* bell chimes, singing on the air as she made camp, still sounded. "A ringing melody, quick and light and lovely. I possess an aural *duoja*," she added. Would Cassende even know what she meant by that? Did Cassende hear the chiming, too?

Cassende nodded. "Yes. The music soothes me, eases the aches in my bones as did the treatment offered in my retreat center in Pavelle."

"Treatment! For troll-disease?" Surely not.

"Yes, for troll-disease."

"There is no such!"

"Minister Gabris Gustiya under the emperador of Giralliya developed one three years before."

Paiam could scarcely credit it. Troll-disease and trolls had plagued the North-lands always. Incurable. Leading to insanity and death. Damaging to anyone encountering them. The Hammarleedings suffered fewer trolls than the lowlanders, but even the mountains were not entirely free of the scourge. If there *were* a cure . . .

"Why are you here, if your cure lies south?"

"The villagers of Osier share your skepticism."

Some memory haunted Cassende's eyes. A hostile mob? Men brandishing staves or blades? Paiam had her own memories of the hunters who had saved her from a troll. What would it be like to stand on the other side of their violence? Renewed pity softened her suspicion.

"They drove you out? Away?"

"Yes." Cassende looked down, pain crossing her face.

"There was no one to take your part," Paiam guessed.

"My husband . . . I think, I know . . . they killed him."

Paiam's breath hissed in. "So civilized, your southern lands."

Cassende's head came up. "What would your neighbors do to a troll-lover?"

"I don't know. Not that, I hope." Kaunis-lodge had never discovered a troll among the sisters. Nor Tukeva-lodge among the brothers. The troll who had threatened Paiam as a child had been a lowlander fled into the mountains. "So you fled north."

"I *fled*. And found myself pressed north. First by my neighbors. Later, by others."

"This far?"

"In Garnhult, I heard the first strains of the antiphonic music and felt its easing of my bones. I followed it."

"*Antiphonic* music? Is that what you call it?"

"The lowlander Silmarish would name it keyholding, I suppose."

Ah, yes, so they would. If the Giralliyans named magic as antiphony, if Giralliyan antiphony were the same as lowlander keyholding, and keyholding were the same as Hammarleeding *duoja*, then perhaps antiphony was the Giralliyan idea of *duoja*. But Cassende heard the same magical melody that sounded in Paiam's ears. It had developed a counterpoint rhythm now, building to some unimaginable crescendo perhaps?

"The music cures your disease?"

"No, alas. It merely eases the pain, but that alone made it worth following."

Cassende finished the last of her broth and set her mug aside. Paiam continued to sip hers. It was cooling to lukewarm.

"What will you do now?"

"That depends upon you and Herralte Dainarspring, does it not? I am your prisoner, no?"

Paiam stifled a sigh. What would she do with Cassende? What would Ivvar do with Cassende? There were no easy answers. Smuggling her south to where treatment was available seemed unlikely to succeed. Too many leagues and too many people to elude. Slaying rabid trolls spitting lethal *incantatio* was one thing. Slaying Cassende . . . no. Finding a hidden hillcot where she could live secluded . . . wouldn't work unless they stayed nearby to bring her provisions regularly. And what would happen when her troll-disease progressed enough to make her dangerous. Gah!

"Do you think the source of the music is near?" Paiam thought it must be. The melody had grown ever more continuous and ever more intense as she followed the trail away from The Mug and Mink.

Cassende nodded.

"Do you think we might find it, if we searched? Now?"

"Oh! Could we? Would you help me?" Cassende's face grew eager. "If I could rest in the heart of it, I almost think I might be cured."

"Really!" If that were so . . . it might be a solution to their dilemma right there. Improbable as it seemed, if there were cures in the south, maybe there were cures in the north as well. Paiam felt the insides of Cassende's boots, positioned with their open tops toward the fire, their laces removed. Still damp, but no longer soaked. If Paiam lent her a pair of waxed silk overhose, Cassende could wear them and still have dry feet.

Ivvar had borrowed Pai's trekking poles so he could run.

And run he did, snowshoes thumping soft on the blanketed ground, poles swinging briskly as he swung his arms, snow-crusted thickets rustling as he plunged through them, bearing north northeast, straight for that faint-but-ominous roaring that sounded again on the still air.

He barely noticed the golden light streaming from the low break in the clouds behind him. He noticed the gold-tinged black tree trunks only enough to avoid them. He ignored entirely the renewed mild ache in his knees that often came at the end of a long and strenuous day.

He still could not pin down any memory of the roaring beast. Frost leopards gave a softer, more spitting cough. Ice tigers, a low, but less prolonged growl. North-bears, a strangely pulsating rumble – *gung gah, gung gah, grr* – almost like swallowed speech. He *knew* this harsh thunder, so low it shook the bones. Couldn't place it, but knew it boded trouble. Worse than trouble. Disaster.

He pushed himself harder.

Surely at a closer vantage point he might see the beast. Or recognize its bellow.

Sweat broke out again on his back, dampening his undertunic and then his already-damp sweater tunic. His pack mashed the clammy fabric against his skin. His nose grew cold from the breeze of his own passage. His breath came in pants.

The smell of wet wool and raw silk rose from his garments to mix with the resinous aroma of the pines and the freshness of cold air.

Were it not for the angry fear growing in his belly, he'd be enjoying himself. Pushing his limits, racing through the winter woodlands on a mission of moment. He reveled in a challenge.

But not now. Not when Paiam stood in harm's way. Not when he'd found her again, found . . . the possibility of something with her again. Now he would have only peace and beauty at hand to present to her. A tame wilderness in which to explore their companionship.

He snorted at the ridiculous juxtaposition. The backcountry was never tame.

The angle of the light from behind him continued to lower. The stripes of the tree trunk shadows grew long, one blending into the next in continuous jagged lines over the flat, flat snow-covered forest floor.

The ground continued flat. Flat. And more flat.

Then suddenly it wasn't.

Ivvar dug Paiam's poles fiercely into the snow, through it into the chilled pine needles below, through the pine needle carpet into the cold earth beneath.

Great gouged swatches of black soil edged by pine needles mixed with snow appeared under the points of the trekking poles.

Ivvar teetered on the brink of a ravine, cursing.

Demons! He should have remembered that the course of the river Iskoldevand took it right across his northeasterly path.

He fell hard on his backside.

But did not go over the brink yawning before the tips of his snowshoes.

The roar of the beast sounded again, echoing long and low across the ravine, vibrating in Ivvar's bones, quivering in his belly.

Ivvar shuddered, the sour taste of dread in his mouth.

A moment later, the roarer eeled above the opposite cliff, crushing trees under its vast serpentine bulk, ripping rock with its gripping claws, ululating from a cavernous and fanged maw.

Ice wyrm.

Gleaming gold in the evening sun, scaled dragon body and muscled dragon limbs, great fringed head with icy lamps for eyes. The cold rolled off its flanks like wind off a blizzard, roiling down into the ravine, and geysering high along the nearer side.

Duoja in her demesne!

Ice wyrm.

Long ago in his youth, before he'd grown strong enough to fight the *onderneming*, he'd seen one of the creatures dying, braying anger at its demise, thrashing and destroying the mountainside in its protest. Ivvar and his brothers watched from across a broad alpine valley, safely distant.

This creature loomed close, twisting its massive head from side to side, raking the forest with its menacing glance.

The sun dipped below the horizon, removing gold from the wyrm's scales. They turned gleaming silver under the sky's pale blue light. Silver and cold, colder than ice, colder than night, colder than the Death Woman the Reindeer People worshipped.

The wyrm's claws flexed and dug, translucent sharpness designed to slice.

The wyrm's maw closed and its beaked snout dove as the long creature eeled into the ravine.

It wasn't even a decision: Ivvar leapt to his feet, sprinting along the ravine's brink, aiming for the natural ramp he'd spotted to his left, the only way in sight down to the river below.

Down to the bottom.

Down to the frozen river.

Down to the wyrm, to intercept it *now*. Here was an *onderneming* to shame them all.

He thrust Pai's trekking poles into the empty loop on his belt, snatched his wooden quilting wand from its pocket in his coat, and began to stitch the air as he descended.

Heat of flame to light a lantern.

Heat of a stove to warm a lodge.

Heat of a bonfire to roast a ram.

Heat of a forest fire to scorch the land.

Heat of Duoja to devour a demon.

He arrived, the abrupt leveling of the slope buckling his knees.

Staggering, he drove his *duoja*-conjured heat through the air like a spear, across the ice-clad river and into the breast of the towering wyrm.

The beast howled.

Ivvar's bones shook within his flesh.

And the wyrm turned, eeling away down the course of the Iskoldevand, the sharp fins of its pointed tail rippling as it disappeared around the bend.

Ivvar reeled, then caught himself.

This was not finished. He'd turned the beast aside, but who knew where it might wander next. He had to return to Paiam and Cassende, guide them to a safer haven.

Climbing back up the natural ramp that he'd descended in such a hurry was much, much harder. He pulled Pai's trekking poles back out of their loop, glad he'd not merely tossed them aside when he needed his hands free. With each step, his bad knee did more than ache; it spasmed.

Dear Duoja, he couldn't be this slow. He had to get back to Pai *quickly*.

Paiam shrugged out of her trapunto-quilted jacket and helped Cassende pull it on over her borrowed sweater-tunic. The troll-woman had managed to pull the oiled silk hose over the thicker knitted ones, as well as getting her damp leather boots on. She'd grinned shyly at Paiam, saying, "I'm glad your wool stockings are thick. My boots are big." Perhaps that had been another factor contributing to her fall.

Paiam had mended the slashed bootlaces with makeshift knots and poked them through the many lacing holes along the leather tongues of the footwear. Cassende tied them deftly enough. Skill transferred from managing the multitude of straps typical of Giralliyan sandals? Paiam wondered. But Cassende had been awkward while struggling with the jacket.

Her bruises, hidden now by undertunic and sweater-tunic and jacket, hampered the movement of her arms.

As Paiam pushed the toggle buttons of her jacket into the loops, a hint of dizziness swayed her.

Just so had she fastened her little daughter's jacket, when Sarvet was five.

Cassende's gloved fingers gripped Paiam's wrist, and her soft gaze grew abruptly keen. "Are you ill, frualte? Or merely weary?"

Paiam finished the last toggle and stepped away.

"No, no. Just a moment of –" a moment of what? "– of memory."

Cassende smiled. "I understand."

No doubt she did. The troll must have her own store of disconcerting remembrances.

The chiming melody that sounded in Paiam's *duoja* sense had paused for an interval. Now it started up again, slower, gentler, but with a sense of greater power behind it. Was the fanfare over? The real work – whatever that was – begun?

Paiam bent to re-fasten her snowshoes, then gathered her hooded cape from the ground cloth and slung it around her shoulders. She pulled her fleece-lined mittens directly over her hands, since Cassende had her silk undergloves.

The *duoja* music sounded as though it came from farther along the trail skirting the clearing, somewhere to the south and west. She pointed with her mittened hand. "That way, don't you think?"

Cassende nodded and gestured for Paiam to precede her.

The thinning cloud cover of early evening had dissipated completely, but the light that lingered so long after sundown in northern skies was all but gone. The sky now glowed the deep indigo blue that heralded the coming dark of night. The evening star – the lamp of Sias – shown just above the tree tops, while a sprinkling of lesser stars pricked out overhead.

The forest was altogether in shadow. They could have traveled nowhere, but for the snow, its whiteness pale on the ground, shedding a cool radiance of its own, silvery like dim moonlight.

Paiam glanced at their camp. Tent waiting, fire banked, wood stacked, groundcloth weighted at its corners. They shouldn't be gone long. She could feel that the *duoja* melody was near, near.

She set out for the trail, Cassende behind her.

The snow crunched under their footsteps, colder, lacking the sun and without the clouds to hold warmth in. A fallen holly limb, thin and twiggy and many-branched, blocked the trail at the edge of the clearing.

Paiam lifted it aside, holding it at arm's length to avoid getting her garments caught in the prickly leaves.

She remembered another walk, long ago in the valley below her home. It was Giving-day, the fete at the end of the fall and the beginning of winter. She was five months pregnant. Ivvar had come to Kaunis-lodge with the Tukeva-men and invited her on a walk. Just as she'd moved this holly branch for Cassende, so he had moved another for her. And just as she had buttoned her jacket onto the troll-woman, so Ivvar had buttoned his onto Paiam.

Snow had blanketed the valley that day with Ivvar so long ago, but the day was mild. She'd forgone her own jacket, not wanting to carry it, not wanting to be overwarm. They'd lingered on their walk, adding a detour to the Terava Rocks to see the frozen waterfall there, gleaming like living pearl in the twilight. With dark coming on, she'd grown cold. Ivvar had laughed and pulled his jacket from his rucksack, wrapping it around her while she gaped in surprise. She'd felt so cared for, so safe. And hated it, because under that safety, she felt vulnerable. If he could make her safe, then he could make her unsafe, too.

I wanted my own strength, not his. Borrowing strength felt risky.

And so she picked a quarrel on their way home.

She couldn't even remember what it had been about. Certainly not the real problem: her sense of vulnerability. But it had been bitter. She'd told him to stay in Tukeva for Other-joy, the next fete-day when the men would visit, and he'd acquiesced, his face sad.

Why had she been so untrusting of her own strength, so convinced that it would melt if she learned to rely on Ivvar's strength?

I was young.

Yes, that was part of it. But it felt like there was more. She'd never really worked it out after Ivvar went to live in Rakas-lodge. He was gone, no longer a threat to her strength. She didn't need to know why he'd been a threat.

What about now? Was her strength at risk now?

He'd departed to investigate a roaring noise so soft that she'd not discerned it, because he feared it might be dangerous. Did she feel weak, because he'd gone and she'd stayed?

No. Not at all.

What had changed? Besides her growing old and experienced and sure of herself deep down in her bones?

Maybe it *was* just age and experience. She'd known weakness with injury and grown strong again. Passed through grief and found happiness again. Nearly lost her daughter in the years of Sarvet's wanderyar, the journey outside the Hammarleeding enclaves taken by many of their young folk. Some of the girls and boys never returned from it. Some lost to perils unknown. Some choosing life among the lowlanders. She'd thought Sarvet might chose so. But she hadn't. She'd returned, and Paiam had rejoiced.

Returning. The return of a loved one. There was the heart of the matter.

Her own dear *mapah* – her father – had departed on Giving-day. Hearty and laughing and tickling her cheeks with his fuzzy gray beard. He'd left her a gift in a carved box for the celebration that would come in Bricember, First-light. When she'd lifted the lid, she'd found a soft toy bear, quilted and stuffed with unspun wool, made for her by him. But he'd been dead a month by then, killed by a burst blood vessel in his head that very day he'd left her.

He'd left and never returned.

Mother hadn't understood. She'd been a comfortable, conventional Hammarleeding woman. Fond of her linking-brother – her husband – yes, but not missing him between fete-days. Content with sisterly companionship and the enjoyable rhythms of life in Kaunis. Paiam's intense grief had bewildered her, and she'd not known how to help.

Paiam grew rigid and devout, seeking solace in worshipping Sias and her champion, Duoja, not understanding that devotion must spring from joy as well as sorrow, from ease as well as pain.

It had all come right in the end. Hadn't it?

Except that Ivvar's required coming and going – the essence of Hammarleeding life, because their men and women lived apart – had felt too fraught to be borne for long.

And yet . . . Ivvar was here now. Well, not here. But nearby. And Paiam felt . . . just fine.

She stopped.

The *duoja* music no longer summoned her forward. Instead, the slow, powerful notes beckoned her off to the side of the trail. She looked over her shoulder, catching Cassende's eye.

The troll-woman stood still, head tilted, listening. Her white hair, the two mounds of it over her ears, gleamed against the darkness under the trees. "It's a birthing, I think," she said.

Yes, Paiam could hear it, too; the rhythm of a woman's labor caught within the melody, expressed by it. Yet no woman labored here in the backcountry with *duoja* as her groans, nor even some beast, whose cubs would arrive in the spring and need no magic.

"This way!" said Cassende, plunging between two pine trunks.

Paiam followed her.

～

Ivvar stumbled as he crested the rim of the ravine bluff, going down painfully on his knees. He struggled up almost at once, staggering forward, attempting to push himself into a run.

With an ice wyrm roaming the wilderness, Pai could be in danger. He couldn't bear to be anywhere but at her side, if the monster threatened her. He would fight it to the last drop of his blood, the last gasp of his breath. He would protect her, preserve her, keep her safe.

But, demons! He couldn't do it walking!

On sheer will alone, he broke into a lumbering jog. The snow, cooling in the dusk, crunched under his careless footsteps. The thongs of his snowshoes creaked with the swing of his heavy stride.

His knee did more than ache. It blazed. And his hip joints commenced a rhythmic throbbing.

Duoja! He was bushed. His hip sockets never ached until he was all in.

He picked up his pace.

Under the light sky of the north's long twilight,

the woods became a blur of smudged shadow as he trampled through them. Not due to his speed, alas – a jog was the most he could manage – but due to his fatigue and his concern.

He could remember another time when he'd hastened to Paiam's side. He'd gotten there, too, even though the Kaunis-mothers frowned on his presence. Hammarleeding women believed childbirth to be a wholly feminine realm. But as the month of Thyril and the birth of their child drew ever closer, Pai had asked him to be there; had begged him. "Can you see me with my mother supporting me through the worst moments?" she'd demanded fiercely.

No, he couldn't see it. Paiam's mother, with her easy laughter and equally easy tears, would collapse under the first stress, leaving Paiam to fight her birthing pains alone, or with the company of someone who didn't care as much.

He'd been at Tukeva when word arrived, of course. And he'd run all the way to Kaunis.

Paiam had crushed his hands and wrists through her sharpest pains, leaving bruise marks on his flesh. He could still hear her furious yells.

She'd clung to his shoulders when the pain ebbed, giving way to the hard work of pushing their baby out of her womb and into the world.

Little Sarvet had been born butt first, not head first like most infants.

He could see her in his mind's eye; her beautiful skin, the luminescent tan of Hammarleeding babies, black fuzz all over her shapely head, and her big, dark, wondering eyes as she lay on Paiam's breast. She was the most lovely she-creature he'd ever adored, except for Paiam, reclining in his arms, radiant in her joy for their daughter.

Yes, he'd been there.

But he'd not been able to protect Paiam from the tragedy that came next.

It wasn't obvious, but when the midwife examined their precious baby, she explained it to them. Sarvet's right hip socket was too shallow, and her breech birth had displaced the ball of the thigh bone ever so slightly, but enough to be a problem. The Kaunis-healers could treat it. And many babies grew better as they grew older and larger.

But it hadn't been that way for Sarvet.

She'd received *duoja* treatments three times every day, but with each leap in her growth, the progress made on deepening the hip socket would be undone. He and Paiam had watched helplessly as the leg turned ever more inward, the thigh muscle shortened, and the limp became more pronounced.

Sarvet herself seemed largely unbothered by her lameness. She developed a sturdy inner fiber, a toughness, that let her enjoy life for what it gave her.

But Paiam blamed him. He blamed himself. Perhaps if they'd conceived their daughter in the proper way, with a sanctified linking under Duoja's auspices rather than a wild night on their own, Sarvet would have been born head first.

Except that was nonsense.

On a different night, a different baby would have been conceived.

He couldn't regret the ecstatic night with Paiam. He couldn't regret their amazing daughter. Sarvet had changed herself and her entire society – making it healthier, he thought – in order to create the life she wanted for herself. Even now, she served as lodge-mother and holy caller in Kaunis-lodge, leading the sisters with her wisdom.

His linking bond with Paiam – his marriage – hadn't survived the physical maiming of their daughter.

But he'd come to understand that the realms of illness and injury were not his battlefield.

The cold that threatened all who dwelt in the mountains? That was his foe, and he fought it back successfully with the *duoja*-imbued coats he made for his brothers.

The *onderneming* who preyed upon the goats and their herders? Those, too, had been his foes.

Ivvar was no healer. He'd failed Pai when a birth injury attacked their daughter. But he would not fail her now, when the *onderneming* threatened her. This was his proper adversary, and he *would* defeat it.

He pushed his jog into a run. He *would* not be too late.

Cassende's moving form was a dark blot of shadow ahead. The troll-woman proved surprisingly deft as she followed a frozen, winding rivulet through the bare, gloom-shrouded pine trunks. Perhaps she was recovering from her ordeal.

The forest floor sloped gently downward, testing Paiam's tired legs. Cassende's head start grew larger, increasing the distance between them.

The *duoja* music sounded in rhythmic surges, sprinkles of notes gathering into a faster intensity that ceased abruptly; then new scintillas embroidered the silence, building to a fresh crescendo.

No earthly creature would birth to such an accompaniment. But this was birth. Unmistakably so. What supernal being would choose ice and cold for its entry into the corporeal world? Could it be one of the pegasi? The mystical winged horses who touched the lives of humans only rarely, but with such life-changing result? Sarvet had met them, and the meeting had shifted the course of her living utterly.

But a pegasus would chose a sun-warmed alpine meadow, not a frozen wilderness, for its advent.

Paiam shivered, remembering her own labor beside the hot tile stove with her sisters around her. She'd been overly hot in her body – although the heat felt good, soothing to her pains – but comfortless and chill in her soul. Until Ivvar arrived. His hands had felt so solid under her grip. His shoulders, so firm when she leaned into him. His focus and his caring, enough to anchor her through her trial.

With his support, she'd made it through.

How might their lives have been different, she wondered, if he'd walked by her side as little Sarvet grew? Lowlander couples lived in the same house for all their days after they married. *I would have liked that.* But Hammarleeding couples did not.

Every Other-joy, the fete celebrating the wonderful connection between a man and a woman, saw the men visiting Kaunis-lodge, but they left for Tukeva at the end of the ritual sequences.

After Long-light in the summer and after Giving-day in the fall, Ivvar left her. Left her and their daughter, bereft without him.

Oh, she'd managed. There were plenty of hands at Kaunis to share the work of rearing a child. Arms to rock a baby, to carry her. Willingness to change a nappy, fetch a teething toy. But none of the sisters loved Sarvet the way Paiam did. Cared the way she did when Sarvet whimpered in pain. Hurt the way she did when Sarvet's limp grew ever worse.

Ivvar had cared. Just as passionately as Paiam did. If she'd had him by her side through it all . . . everything would have been different. She was convinced of that.

Instead, the hinge of feeling within her wound tighter and tighter, while her stores of patience and serenity grew ever more scarce. She'd dissolved her linking-bond to Ivvar. And nearly destroyed her birth-bond with her daughter.

Paiam winced. Those had been dark days. But her days were light now, and had been for tens of years. Life was full and interesting and free of the angst that had plagued her early adulthood.

She bent her head, smiling, and bumped into Cassende. The troll-woman had stopped while Paiam's attention wandered.

Paiam looked up to a clear view over Cassende's short height.

They had come to a small dell in the forest, a dimple fringed with snowy bushes and reindeer moss, a low outcropping of rock presiding over it with a hanging tapestry of ice glistening from the lip of the scooped-out stone. The traceries of frozen water gleamed softly in the night.

Paiam could imagine the glade in summer, feathered with ferns, spicy scents on the air, the echo of moving water thrilling the ear. Duoja herself might bathe in such a haven, her arms splashed by the flowing spring and dappled by sun, her eyes alight with joy in the forest beauty.

As Paiam gazed, seeing the snow-cloaked dell overlain by the imagined sunlit one, the moon rose above the trees to her left.

The muted dove-gray of the snow beamed suddenly bright against the dark twigs of the bushes and the lichen-blotched rock. The pearlescent gleam of the ice curtain flashed into sparkling brilliance, a coruscation of crystal and glinting rainbows, almost alive in the serpentine twists of the cold-locked water and the glistening light.

This, this marvel of wrought ice, was the source of the mystery *duoja*.

Cassende stared at the living tapestry of ice, the subtle gleams of soft rose and gray-blue on its inner curves, brilliant silver along its raised crescents, an aurora of rainbow glints shining from its upper reaches.

It reminded her of a bas relief naiad she'd once created in enameled metals, using her antiphony to shape the medium.

She'd been an artist, respected by her peers, admired by her neighbors. Before her son's accident and the blood poisoning that threatened him. Before she'd pushed her antiphony too far, pushed it into *incantatio.* Saving him, yes, but dooming herself to troll-disease.

The naiad had been the last of her artistic works. Her troll-disease demanded that she become reclusive, hiding her slowly changing features – twisted by the disease – away from the public. She'd hoped to return to her artistry, if the southern treatment restored her sufficiently. She'd missed it. Not enough to regret saving her son. But she did miss it.

She could almost discern a naiad in this arras of frozen water. There was the graceful bend of an arm; there, the long line of an extended leg; and there, the lithe beauty of the slender waist.

She peered more closely at the hint of form. Why, there was the exquisite profile with tilted nose and large eye and high cheekbone! An ice maiden danced within the ice.

Cassende's eyelids fluttered closed as she focused on the chiming music to which the dancer moved. Her antiphonic senses came alive without her willing, deepening her perception of the crystalline notes bathing the air.

The ache in Cassende's bones subsided. A feeling of wellbeing rose through her heels. The crown of her head lifted while the base of her spine straightened. A flutter of faint wing beats shivered along her arcs – the energetic pathways connecting her core to her limbs – the beginning flow of her own antiphony, the safe magic, not the dangerous *incantatio*.

Ah! It felt good, so good.

The wing beats strengthened into a pulsing rhythm.

She opened her eyes, certain there was something new to see.

And there was.

The silvery energy body of – not a naiad, a water spirit – but related to the beings of water, an *ilmatar*, an ice spirit. The ice spirit echoed the blurred form in the ice sculpture, more refined, more detailed, a maiden of cool light dancing in the forest of the night, dancing her way into being.

"Frualte," Cassende whispered. "The ice is birthing a child, a child embodied of the cold freshness of winter, one of the *ilmatari*. Do you know them?"

The Hammarleeding woman's answer came in a low murmur over Cassende's shoulder. "Our legends name them the two-faced ones, born to dance as spirit, or to ravage as wyrm. Depending on how the ice shapes itself under its thawing and re-freezing."

"Can you see her?" asked Cassende.

"Give me a moment to open my *duoja* sense."

Cassende waited, imbibing the beauty of the antiphonic music and the grace of the dancing ice spirit. The ache in her own bones ebbed away completely to be replaced by an invigorated strength. Was the birth of the *ilmatar* healing her troll-disease? Perhaps. Perhaps not. But it felt lovely.

"Look at her nether limbs," came Paiam's low voice. "Notice that they appear as a woman's legs one instant, a snake's tail the next."

Cassende relaxed into her antiphony more completely. Yes, she could see the strange wavering. Serpent's tail. Womanly legs. Serpent's tail.

"I can influence this," she muttered. "I must." An ice wyrm would bring grievous harm were one to spawn here.

Paiam's breath sighed on the shadowed air. "How?"

"Watch me," Cassende instructed. "With your –" what had she called it? *duoja*? "– with your *duoja*-sense."

"I'm watching," breathed her companion.

Delicately, Cassende opened her radices – the gateways in her body to the antiphonic energy – allowing the pulse of it to strengthen still more and flow out through her hands to greet the curves of the ice tapestry, shaping the blurred image toward the maiden she'd initially perceived: the curve of the upraised arm, the grace of the extended leg, the turn of the slender waist.

After a moment, she heard a mellow tone, like a bow-drawn cello, sound from behind her – Paiam's *duoja* – and felt the *duoja*-power join her antiphony in stroking the ice sculpture toward the form of a maiden.

Softly, Cassende began to sing.

"Be ye, be ye born in truth.

Be ye, be ye lovely.

Be ye, be ye born in love.

Be ye most beloved.

Only meeting joy and mirth.

Only loving rapture.

Be ye, be ye born in bliss.

Be ye born to nurture."

Paiam joined her, humming harmony to her melody.

As they sang, the *ilmatar's* silvery energy body stabilized as a maiden.

With each jolting step forward, Ivvar's knee stabbed him, while the ache in his hip sockets throbbed more intensely. Despite his body's fatigue, Ivvar pushed his pace. The long twilight had flowed on through dusk to nightfall. Winking stars shone in the deep cobalt dome of the sky, and the snow-cloaked land glimmered pale. Time was passing more swiftly than he could run, especially in the dark.

He opened his *duoja*-sense. The currents of the land's latent energies would help him avoid gullies and tree trunks and would guide him to his goal.

Ah! The *duoja* of the back country felt like a spring breeze, cool and bracing, but rich with the fragrance of moist loam and stirring roots and rising sap. It wrapped around his weariness and blew it away. His stride steadied and strengthened, growing less ragged and more regular.

He noticed the trace of a snow possum eddying to his left. The fainter residue of muskrat faded at his right. The pines seemed taller, more exaggeratedly vertical. The snow gleamed brighter, assumed a more inviting essence. This was the world with *duoja*: more welcoming, but more intense. He could *feel* the slow wheel of the stars, even though his eyes could not mark their glacial movement.

The breeze of his own passage felt sharper, raising his alertness.

He'd found his rhythm now.

The black columns of the pines flicked by him like drum beats.

The white-blanketed underbrush flowed like ocean waves.

He could go on like this for as long as it took to reach Pai.

He would not stop. He would not falter. He would get there in time.

The moon rose just behind his left shoulder, flooding the woods with silver dapples of light. The gray sheen of the snow brightened to brilliant white. The soft shadows of the trees hardened to coal black. The stirring of the night air picked up. Or did it?

This wasn't the breeze.

This was *duoja*, yet again.

A delicate zephyr of scent and sweetness rising before him, as though a flower bloomed, its petals breathing forth a clean, cool, green aroma that lifted the heart and invigorated the limbs.

Ah!

Could this be the source of the melodies that Paiam had mentioned? Her *duoja* was aural, manifesting in sound, while his disclosed itself via scent and touch and heat and cold.

Pai had named her melody heavenly. This *duoja* breeze smelled heavenly.

Ivvar adjusted his course, aiming just southwest of the clearing where he'd left Paiam and Cassende, moving toward the origin point of the *duoja*. He'd been too distracted by warming the troll-woman and then hearing the ice wyrm to perceive this other anomaly, but it too deserved investigation. Too much strangeness invested this place and this day. And strangeness could herald either good or bad. Best to be prepared for whatever came. Preparedness had ever been his rule; he would not change it now.

He increased his pace yet again, fortified by the energizing *duoja* and his own curiosity.

What would he find? Would Pai be there, too? Somehow he suspected she would be, drawn by her own code of foresightedness and inquiry.

He grinned. Dear Pai - keen minded, passionate, alive, and engaged – he wanted her in his life again, in his days, in his celebrations, in all that came to him. Might she feel the same?

"I'll never mind again," she'd said. It seemed a promising omen. She wasn't the type to speak frivolously, and the words had come from somewhere deep within her. There was hope in that.

The *duoja*-breeze ahead of Ivvar strengthened and acquired more depth to its aroma, greener, less floral, cooler. He breathed it in, glorying in the cold fullness of it. Glorious! Yes, it was glorious! He could feel the newness of its essence permeating his bones, almost bringing the freshness of youth to his age. Was Cassende feeling it too? How might it affect her disease? Favorably, surely. That would be a good thing, while he and Pai pondered how best to help her. Helping her . . . would not be easy. He snorted softly. No, not easy at all, if it were even possible.

The *duoja*-breeze strengthened again and then swung around, blowing from over his left shoulder.

It strengthened yet more, gusting fiercely, with an edge to its bite and a deeper cold to its essence. What in the north? It was a different breeze altogether: harsh and dangerous and aggressive. And yet it was the same: cool and clean and breathing of snowfall.

Abruptly he knew.

The ice wyrm had turned, just as he feared it might. Turned to chase him, to challenge him, to defeat him.

Or was he, indeed, its target?

He stopped his own furious rush, digging in Pai's trekking poles to come to a halt.

He faced the onslaught of the new *duoja*-wind, tasting it, testing it, seeking greater discernment.

Ah! not him. Something ahead of him; something young and fresh; something delicate and beguiling. Ivvar's knowing leapt forward again. The creator of the *duoja*-breeze – which remained present; he could sense it still – beckoned the creator of the *duoja*-wind. So like they were, in their cool freshness. So unlike they were in their character: healing versus destroying.

Which meant – *Duoja and all her demons!* – the ice wyrm was headed for Paiam. Directly for Paiam. Because Paiam was there with the *duoja*-breeze. He knew it as certainly as if he could see her now. And the wyrm would get there before he could. *Demons be damned!*

He spun back around and dove forward, running in a flat-out sprint.

He only thought he'd been pushing before.

Now he was giving it all he had and more.

Even as he pounded through the forest, a groaning roar rumbled through the air. The beast was trumpeting its advent. Still behind him, but not far. Not nearly far enough.

He moved his legs faster.

Sweat dripped down his face. One hot rivulet flowed over the corner of his open, gasping mouth. Its salt taste flooded his tongue.

He forced his knees higher, his stride longer.

A whippy branch cut his cheek, dumped a load of snow in his face. The chill felt good. The momentary blindness, infuriating.

He dashed a hand over his eyes, clearing his sight.

His heart hammered in his chest.

I'll get there! I'll get there! I'll get there!

And then he was there, or nearly there.

He could feel the strong pliancy that was Paiam's *duoja*. He could feel the gentle warmth that must be Cassende's. And he could feel the delicacy of the *duoja*-breeze.

The next moment he burst into a tiny clearing, a small dell in the forest where a flashing, glinting curtain of sculptured ice flowed from a low bluff. A *duoja*-being, formed of silvery light, danced before the ice, all grace and beauty and tenderness.

Illumination burst upon Ivvar's thoughts, and he dropped Pai's trekking poles.

One of the *ilmatari*.

Of course!

Two-faced.

Ice-spirit or ice wyrm. Which would this become?

No wonder the devouring wyrm sped this way!

Ivvar lunged forward to break and destroy.

Break the ice sculpture.

Destroy the *ilmatar*.

Dissipate the beguiling call that summoned the wyrm.

And prevent another wyrm from forming.

He swung his arm in a furious, smashing arc.

Some moments before Ivvar's turbulent entrance, Paiam let the last note of her harmony linger, a sweet resonance on the moonlit air.

Was the forest warmer from her *duoja*? From Cassende's Giralliyan antiphony?

The resinous fragrance of the pines seemed stronger, and the trees held a listening presence.

As Paiam watched over Cassende's shoulder, the ice spirit emerged from her inward focus to see her surroundings for the first time.

She gazed upward to the snowy, needle-fringed branches of pines framing the starry night sky and the full moon. Awe brushed her glowing face. She glanced down at her feet, noting the snow-sprinkled reindeer moss in the dell where she stood. She looked up to meet Paiam's eyes and smiled.

She bowed, a leg forward with foot pointed, one arm forward in a curve, the other swept to the side. Then she began a slower dance – an elegant pavane – circling the dell while moving farther from the ice sculpture.

What was she doing? Was there more to the spirit's birth than this? Did she remain anchored to the ice that created her?

Paiam scrutinized the slow circling of the *ilmatar*. Her beauty of form and of movement was matched by a growing aura of loving kindness. Paiam felt her breath catch with the force of it. She stared, held motionless herself by the wonder of it, yet feeling that she was missing something.

She lifted the crown of her head and allowed the base of her spine to sink, relaxing into a straighter posture, relaxing more deeply into her own *duoja*.

Aaah! The gossamer glimmer of a rainbow film of light spread from the ice sculpture outward, swirling around the *ilmatar* in a spiraling garment, so faint that Paiam's *duoja*-sense could barely perceive it.

As Paiam concentrated, she heard a crashing sound in the woods behind her – the passage of something large through the underbrush – followed by a low, groaning roar at a greater distance.

Ivvar's beast?

An instant later, Ivvar himself burst from between the trees.

He dove for the ice sculpture, a grimace of desperation on his face, his arm sweeping in from the side with the single intent to smash the delicate tapestry.

Paiam flung herself before him, reaching for his arm to knock it aside.

Ivvar crashed into her, chest to chest.

She felt herself falling.

Ivvar's arm circled her waist, gripping her as he changed the direction of their momentum. She felt herself swung around and up. Then she landed with a thump, Ivvar beneath her, cushioning her fall.

She scrambled to her feet, standing over him, abruptly furious.

"How dare you!" she demanded.

This was just like when their daughter was little. He'd been absent while the ice spirit coalesced. As he'd been absent through Sarvet's young years. "Never there to see the struggle. Never there to share the burden. Never there to share the joy. Never. Blasted. There!"

She realized she was yelling only when she saw the confusion in his face give way to anger.

His anger was quieter than hers. It always had been.

"You sent me away." He sat up slowly, his eyes holding hers.

That was true. She had dissolved their linking-bond. She had asked him to skip some of the fete-days. She had insisted he cease to approach her when he did visit Kaunis-lodge.

But she'd wanted the exact opposite. For him to flout Hammarleeding conventions just as he had when he courted her. For him to arrive early and leave late. For him to visit when no visit was sanctioned. For him to never leave at all.

"Dear Duoja," she murmured faintly. She'd never admitted the truth to herself. No wonder their relationship had never worked. How could it, when she was lying to both herself and to him? How could they ever have settled their differences, lacking a foundation of truth?

Ivvar got his feet under him and pushed slowly up to standing, holding Paiam's eyes all the while.

"I wanted to stay with you, by your side, *on* your side. I wanted this more than I wanted anything." His voice broke on the last word, but from anger – however quiet in its tenor – not from grief.

"I wanted you there," Paiam murmured.

Ivvar's wrath left his face. "Dear Pai, the *ilmatar* is summoning an ice wyrm. Now do you see . . . ?"

Duoja in her demesne.

"An ice wyrm? That roaring?"

She felt her stomach sinking. An ice wyrm. *Demesne above!* How could they survive the mere arrival of such a creature? Vast, powerful, predatory.

They were doomed. Yet she could not countenance the deliberate destruction of the ice spirit, not even for self-preservation. Such destruction would be murder.

She stepped closer to Ivvar, stretching out her hands. He took them in his. She shook her head.

"Ivvar, the *ilmatar* is healing Cassende. You mustn't destroy it."

His eyes widened and left hers, looking behind her. She turned slightly to follow his gaze.

Cassende had not ceased her antiphony when Paiam ceased her singing. Instead of magically shaping the ice sculpture, she appeared to be caressing the air with broad sweeps of her arms.

Paiam could no longer perceive the rainbow gauze connecting the *ilmatar* to her ice – it had faded from her *duoja* sense – but she knew it swirled in its spiral, and knew that Cassende addressed it.

She could hear the troll-woman's continuing magic, a steady vibrato just below the threshold of sound.

Cassende herself looked transfigured, younger, stronger, and enraptured, although her coiled hair remained white.

Ivvar's grip firmed on Paiam's hands, drawing her attention back to him.

"Do you understand, Pai? An ice wyrm?"

The creature's roar sounded, nearer than before.

Paiam felt tears start from her eyes. She stared into Ivvar's face, so familiar, so unfamiliar, but still loving her, after all these years. Could *he* understand?

"Ivvar, please. Do you see her? See them both? See Cassende healing? See the *ilmatar* becoming?" She had to make him understand. How could she? She'd never been able to make him understand before. Of course, she had not tried before; not properly.

His face softened. He raised her hands to his lips and kissed the back of each in turn.

The ice wyrm roared again, nearer yet.

"Duoja in her demesne," murmured Ivvar. He squeezed her fingers one last time, then let them go. "Ready yourselves!" He raised his voice to include Cassende in this direction.

His pack already lay on the ground.

With quick precision, he untied his snowshoes and kicked them off.

Then he drew not his long knife, but his pointed quilting wand, carved of mountain ash and normally used in the filling of trapunto designs.

Paiam winced. What was she asking when she asked Ivvar to preserve the *ilmatar*? His death? Her own? For a miracle to appear?

Ivvar took one last look at Paiam.

There she stood in the moonlight, tall and straight and strong in her Hammarleeding tunic and leggings. The ewe headpiece of her cape had fallen back, revealing the elegant tilt of her head, crowned by the long braid encircling it. The crow's feet around her eyes stood out, but her eyes themselves looked young and filled with determination. That was his Pai: undefeatable. And yet she seemed more flexible than of old, more capable of humor, even in this fraught moment.

Then he plunged into the woods, and she was gone from his sight.

The lumps of the forest floor made themselves felt through the snow and through the pliable soles of his boiled wool boots. His snowshoes provided more comfort for long trekking through the wilderness, but his boots would give him surer footing for a fight.

The roar of the ice wyrm rumbled up ahead, stirring the marrow of his bones.

He studied the trees around him. They were tall and wide of girth, part of an old-growth grove. This would be a good place to make a stand, were it not so close to the *ilmatar's* dell. The size and strength of the ice wyrm could break slenderer trees almost casually with the force of its passage. Ivvar would be threatened by both falling timber and the greater freedom that his foe had to move in a younger cluster of pines.

Amidst these old giants, the wyrm would have to thread its way. Nor would it have a clear swing for its massive clawed limbs or the muscular whip of its tail. Ivvar could use the tree boles as a shield from the wyrm's strikes.

He eased forward more slowly, checking the spacing of the trees – closer was better – and vigilant for the arrival of this largest of the *onderneming*.

The wyrm roared again, louder this time, buffeting Ivvar's ears and rattling his joints.

As the bellow subsided, Ivvar saw it, the fringed lower jaw poised above the snow at man-height, a taloned claw flexed against a tree trunk, the other gripping the ground.

The creature's pale, pale eye skewered Ivvar.

Then it lunged forward, faster than Ivvar had dreamed it could, powerful legs driving the wyrm at speed, serpentine body whipping through the pine boles. It loomed large in an instant, the vast flank curving above Ivvar's head, a burning cold streaming off the silver scales.

Ivvar leapt away, tucking in a roll to gain more ground and arriving behind one of the widest pines in the glade.

The ice wyrm recovered from its rush and turned, crashing against a massive tree trunk that quivered under the impact, but did not break.

Pull yourself together, Ivvar told himself. He'd wasted a moment gawking, and he'd not survive that mistake more than once. His foe was wily and fast.

Sliding rapidly backward, he began quilting the air, gathering his *duoja* like unspun wool, pooling heat in a mass.

Glowing coals.

Flowing lava.

Molten bronze.

Demon's tongues.

Gathering fire, pooling incandescence, concentrating an inferno.

Retreating all the while, canny in his steps, unshaken by the wyrm's writhing rushes.

Back.

And back.

Then a stand as his foe surged forward, an overwhelming wave of bulk and power.

Ivvar released his scorching *duoja*, channeling the flare into a piercing thrust at the wyrm's breast, aiming for the icy heart of the beast that legend claimed as the origin of its life.

The wyrm roared. Its scouring blast knocked Ivvar from his feet, slamming him against a pine bole.

The breath punched from his body, and he felt his ribs creak.

The wyrm's claw swerved toward him, and he thought he was done for.

But it veered abruptly away, drawn by a *duoja* not his: pliable like a woven cord, strong like braided wire, unbreakable like fluid water. Paiam! Not physically at his side, but magically part of the fight.

She was wielding her *duoja*-crook – the skill she used to lure the wild sheep down from the mountaintops in the spring and again in the autumn – forcing the ice wyrm to do her bidding.

Ivvar levered himself up. Now he had a chance.

He and Pai were awkward allies at first, never having done this before, and too distant – not even within sight – to coordinate via speech. They were guessing.

He baited his foe, slipping from tree to tree, ignoring his bruises. Stitching heat via his trapunto wand, waiting for opportunity, daring the wyrm's lethal proximity to loose his attack.

Paiam saved him at the last moment, again and again.

His body would be black and blue all over, like Cassende's, if he survived this.

Their guesses grew better, she retarding the wyrm to open it for Ivvar's strike. Ivvar anticipating her influence on his foe.

They began to develop a rhythm. He would wait on her, then strike. She would wait on him, then pull.

Strike.

Dodge.

Leap.

Heave.

Ivvar's body felt loose and strong – the tired aches almost a separate awareness, belonging to someone else. He could prowl, he could spring, he could thrust, he could recede. He could fight forever with Pai on his side.

The exultant Ivvar fought.

Another Ivvar throbbed with injured pain.

And a third Ivvar reveled in this partnership with his beloved.

Paiam's *duoja* flowed and flickered and flashed around him, clear and clean in its essence. This was what he'd longed for in their linking. This was what he'd hoped for in their lives together.

For the first time he felt his grief from the past. He'd not felt it – not fully – when she bade him leave her. He'd understood her too well, perceived her pain too intensely, been too eager to forgive her. Now his memories pierced him. He had lost the people most precious to him, his linking-sister and his daughter, lost them forever. It had been devastating. He'd been devastated, but never really claimed it.

Now he was claiming it.

The grief felt like a spear through his heart. The grieving felt like stone crushing his chest.

This was his. His to own. His to suffer. His to accept.

His.

And his to release.

He felt it go, cleaving from him like one of his own thrusts into the wyrm.

He was light as air, light as light, light as *duoja*.

Peace rushed in to fill the space occupied only a moment before by heavy, painful sorrow.

This was true forgiveness. Not cloying and sad like the facsimile he'd offered Paiam before, but free and joyous the way it should be. Paiam didn't need his pity. She never had. His pity had injured her as much as her fear had injured him. They could leave both sins behind and move forward unencumbered.

Ivvar delivered a thrust to the wyrm like no other he'd managed before in this long, scrambling fight through the forest.

For the first time, he saw it flinch from him.

The dell around Paiam glowed in the moonlight, forgotten by her.

The sweet fragrance of the pines perfumed the air, equally forgotten.

The beauty of the *ilmatar* coalesced, forgotten.

Cassende's intriguing magic – antiphony – progressed. Forgotten.

All Paiam's concentration focused on her *duoja*-sense and Ivvar's enemy, feeling the corrosive ire of the ice wyrm, predicting its next attack on Ivvar, jerking her *duoja*-crook tight to hinder the monster as it lunged.

For the ice wyrm was no ewe to bow to her herding.

The wild sheep of the mountains relished their freedom, and she partook of their innocent joy when she slipped her *duoja*-sense into their consciousness. The wild rams fought her control fiercely, but submitted wholly in a surrender that she found ecstatic. Luring the wild herd fulfilled her as no other religious ritual could.

Luring the ice wyrm was nothing like that.

Its wrath burned like the scouring ice flung by winter's most bitter blizzard.

Its submission lasted only moments before it fought free, and she must recapture its will.

Its fierce obsession with destruction bruised her heart.

None of these sensations brought pleasure.

Paiam feared she'd failed dozens of times before she caught and followed Ivvar's rhythm. Feared each time she felt him fall that he'd fail to rise. Feared each time she felt the wyrm strike that it struck true.

Duoja help me, she prayed, unaware that she did so. *Let me be a champion like you.*

When she and Ivvar began to fight in concert – by design more often than by accident – it felt better. The first time they managed to trick the wyrm felt marvelous. *Yes! We can do this!*

Ivvar landed three solid blows with his heat-*duoja*, and Paiam felt the wyrm flinch.

Was it possible that they might seize victory out of this mishmash of an unplanned defense?

Crazy. It was crazy. And yet it felt so right: she and Ivvar together, pursuing their goal as partners, sensing one another's rhythm and adding to it. This was what their linking-bond was meant to be. This was what they'd missed when they failed to make it work.

This was what she'd destroyed, when she permitted fear to control her outlook, fear to rule her choices, fear to counsel retreat.

How much had it hurt him? Hurt Ivvar?

He'd never told her. Never castigated her. Never blamed her.

Merely set her free – and set himself free – when the pain eclipsed all else.

For an instant she relived it: the soul-crushing wound of losing him.

And then relived it again. From his point of view.

Her heart ached. *Ivvar, dear Ivvar, how could I have hurt you so?*

Never again. She would hurt no one again out of fear.

Mistakes? Oh, yes, she would make them and hurt herself and others because of them.

Sheer selfishness? Oh, yes, she was not immune. It would happen from time to time.

Weariness? Ignorance? Short-sightedness? Yes, yes. Duoja was a saint. Paiam was not.

But never again fear. She had feared enough for three lifetimes. She'd paid her dues on that one. With fear, she was done.

She heard Ivvar shouting wordlessly as he thrust a potent strike home.

Heard him? With her ears?

Dear Duoja!

Abruptly her surroundings piled in on her senses.

The stillness of the snowy dell around her. The resinous aroma of the pines. Cassende's rapt and now-motionless concentration. The equally enraptured *ilmatar,* paused in her dance to dream.

And the crashing sounds of bushes broken, the creaking of tree trunks bent.

Duoja in her demesne!

She and Ivvar had learned how to fight the ice wyrm. Learned how to press their attack. But they had not guided the path of the struggle.

Crack!

One of the smaller trees at the edge of the dell snapped, spewing shards of wood and crashing down beside Cassende.

The ice wyrm coiled out from the gap, charging.

Not aimed at gentle Cassende. Nor at tall Paiam. Straight for the ice-fall pouring over the bluff.

The wyrm's massive claw plunged down.

The ice tapestry shattered.

And then Paiam *duoja*-noosed the wyrm again.

Just a scant instant too late for the *ilmatar*.

Deep in her antiphonic magic, Cassende heard the ice filigree shatter.

The thumping *crump* of the wyrm's claw coming down.

A metallic crash – like a brass cymbal – fracturing the air.

The attenuating vibration that oscillated loud and soft and loud again after the wreckage.

The trampling bulk of the wyrm barreled through the dell – its shoulder jarring the crest of the bluff loose and tumbling the rock, its tail uprooting another sapling pine – but the disruption felt superficial compared to the essential injury done within the antiphonic energy.

Cassende breathed in the resinous odor of the freshly broken tree without noticing it, her full focus on the spirit of the ice. The moment stretched, still and dark with the *ilmatar* the only brightness in it.

As the echo of destruction swung – in and out and in – Cassende saw the spiral gauze that had been condensing around the *ilmatar* reverse it's flow, spreading and shredding. The ice spirit's face clenched, agonized.

What could Cassende do? Oh, *balance*, but she wanted to do *something*. The ice spirit was dying.

The dissipating rainbow gossamer thinned and thinned and then reversed again, spiraling back toward the ilmatar in the form of a rope. The shock of its connection brought the ice maiden to her knees.

Abruptly, Cassende understood what she was perceiving.

One end of the rainbow strand anchored in the *ilmatar's* essence.

The other rooted in the wyrm, voracious and devouring, bent on consuming. The *ilmatar* was its treasure, oh, yes, but a treasure to be eaten, not safeguarded.

Cassende's son had nearly perished and she'd saved him. This moment felt like that one: healing and beauty and kindness on the cusp, just as Stefano's innocence and verve and warmth – her darling child – had swayed before final extinction.

Cassende reached within herself to the founts of her magic, the radices at the seven focus points – root, belly, plexus, heart, throat, brow, and crown – that floated because of her troll-disease. Healthy radices were anchored. Troll radices drifted. But even troll radices supplied magic. She reached, reached again, and pulled.

The acrid orange light of *incantatio* flashed around her.

She heard herself yelling – probably the doggerel poetry that went with troll-magic – but did not recognize the words.

Her hands stiffened, her fingers pointed.

The searing orange light converged into a blade. It passed through the strand connecting wyrm and spirit, severing it.

The rainbow coil rebounded.

Rebounded again.

Cassende caught it with her hands.

The strand burst into a confetti of rainbow scintillas, a delicate cloud of flickering light and subtle melody, and then converged on her diseased body.

Her consciousness rested for a moment in two places: its proper home – herself – and the energy body of the *ilmatar*.

For that moment, she *was* the *ilmatar*.

She felt cool and clear like northern water.

Fresh and free like northern wind.

Shining and perfect like northern ice.

She was elemental, glorying in the physical sensations of destiny fulfilled, untroubled by the emotions and connections of humanity. This was the harmony and oneness taught in Giralliyan retreats. She would never be the same again.

The next moment, she was the *ilmatar* being Cassende.

Feeling the surge and tug of muscles, the ache of bruises, for the first time.

Suffering the paradox of wanting two opposite things at the same instant.

Exploring the mundanity and the joy and the muddle that was the love of one human for another.

And glorying in it.

Understanding that she had found the ultimate fount of being. Knowing that she would never be the same again.

A laugh stuttered from Cassende's lips even as she stood transfixed in a double enlightenment.

Unable to move, unable to worry, she felt the *ilmatar* probe into her troll-woman's bones, sliding along the arcs that connected her radices. The shock when the spirit touched Cassende's root radix brought her to her knees.

They mirrored one another, spirit and troll. Kneeling, astonished, exalted.

Then the *ilmatar* gripped that which she touched.

Cassende's root radix moved, and Cassende felt turned inside out.

It should have hurt, but it didn't.

It should have been excruciating, but it wasn't.

Her root radix moved and moored itself in the location where it belonged, the root point of a healthy woman, no longer floating as it had, as it did in a troll.

Cassende felt her chest shaken with sobs, her face wet with tears, and the *ilmatar* proceeded from one radix to the next, leaving each perfectly configured in her wake.

Then it was done.

Cassende came back to herself, staring at the ice spirit staring at her.

"Thank you," she whispered.

The spirit smiled, then flowed to her feet with a grace that surpassed even her earlier loveliness. She was more translucent than before, almost transparent, almost invisible. This was the *ilmatar's* proper form. Proper in essence and yet wholly different, Cassende knew. This *ilmatar* would not forget her experience of humanity and transcendence.

The spirit pirouetted once, bowed, and stepped lightly out of the dell that had sheltered her birth.

A new melody started, the patter of spring rain on water, sprightly and quiet at once.

The dark forest folded her in, but her music lingered on the air, fading as she danced away.

Then silence.

Silence.

And silence.

And then a distant crashing, as of some vast monster retreating through the woods, compelled by superior force.

Cassende smiled.

The ice wyrm would follow the *ilmatar* forever, but no longer as the hunter. The hunter had succumbed to the snare.

Ivvar lay at the base of a pine. The tree's straight bole beside his head rose up like a pillar in a vast temple to the night sky, spangled with stars, the moon riding high, and fringed with pine needles on the branches so far above.

It took a while before Ivvar noticed what he was seeing.

His ribs ached as though a cloud giant had used him as a punching bag. His knees felt three times their proper size, pulpy and hot. His hip sockets throbbed as though bruised.

Cassende's worried face swam into his vision.

"'M alive," he mumbled.

"Can you sit?" she asked.

He couldn't. Not at first.

"Are your ribs broken?" she wanted to know.

He lifted his right hand. The quilting wand hung broken from his fingers, the wood snapped in two by his last fall and dangling by a splinter. There was a shame. It had survived the whole fight intact and yielded only upon the wyrm's . . . defeat? Departure? He was a little muddled.

He let the wand fall, probing his flanks with his fingertips.

Ah, but that hurt!

"Not broken," he managed. "Bruised. I think."

"That's good."

Cassende looked remarkably well herself. Ivvar studied her while he gathered himself for another try at sitting. Her delicate prettiness seemed less frail. She stood straighter, held her head with its coils of silver hair higher. If it were daylight, he'd probably see color in her cheeks. The calm stillness that seemed inherent in her held a contentment that she had lacked before. He wondered how that had come to pass. What part had she played in the recent conflict? An important one, he was sure.

"Will you try again?" she urged.

He nodded.

Turning away from the tree trunk . . . wasn't going to work. That was where the worst bruising on his ribs was located. Sitting straight up, calling on abused belly muscles, felt equally unthinkable. He'd have to roll the other way, even if it meant mashing his face into tree bark.

It did, but he managed it; achieving the side position and then pushing up from the roots. He leaned back against the tree, dizzy, but sitting.

"Would you like some water?" Cassende's still center was restful. Duoja be blessed that she wasn't the hysterical sort. He couldn't deal with hysteria just now.

He reached for the water canteen that she'd removed from his belt.

"The cork is out," she warned.

The water tasted like heaven, like Duoja's love, like sunrise after a night of dread. So cool, so soothing, as it flowed down his ragged throat, shouted hoarse in the fight.

"Thanks." His mouth corners turned up in a tired smile.

Motion from the dell, visible through the trees, caught his attention.

Paiam staggered from one trunk to the next, exhausted, but not injured. Was that right? Not injured? A strand of her gray hair – wooly-textured like his own – hung down beside her face, escaped from her braided coronet. Her sweater-tunic looked rumpled; a rip tattered the knee of her leggings; her cape hung back to front, the ewe hood dangling against her breast.

She fetched up next to Cassende, who put an arm around the taller woman's waist, offering support.

They all three spoke at once.

"Pai! Dear Pai, I'd have died without you."

"We won, Ivvar! The three of us together. We prevailed!"

"Steady, steady now, frualte. Keep your feet!"

Paiam did keep her feet, but getting Ivvar to his was a chore. Paiam and Cassende weren't strong enough – and Cassende was too short – to pull his long, rangy body up by the arms. Plus it would have hurt his ribs too much. He couldn't pull himself up by gripping the branch of a nearby sapling for the same reason. In the end, he got on all fours and pushed up while Pai and Cassende each hauled at a hip bone from behind.

"The wyrm?" asked Ivvar, his balance wavering.

Paiam answered, "Gone."

An odd expression crossed Cassende's face. "It sought to tie the *ilmatar* to it. To drink her beauty down until there was none left."

Ivvar stared at her, noticing that Paiam's lips had parted too.

"So that was why . . . what would it have done if the *ilmatar* had evolved into a wyrm rather than an ice maiden?" Ivvar wondered.

Cassende shook her head. "I severed the antiphonic cord with which it had captured her, and then all it could do was follow her in longing."

Ivvar blinked. There was a sketch to beguile the eye. He pictured it: the ice spirit dancing away through the forest while the wyrm eeled after her like a forlorn kitten. A brief laugh puffed air out his nostrils. His ribs twinged. Ow!

So they owed their deliverance to Cassende. He and Paiam had merely occupied the ice wyrm long enough for Cassende to rescue the *ilmatar*. And then the *ilmatar* saved them all.

Ivvar took a ginger step away from the pine trunk.

And nearly yelled. Demons! Would his left knee ever recover?

On the next step, his right knee hurt just as much.

Perhaps labeling his fight as "merely" anything was understating it too much.

Paiam left Cassende's support to wedge her shoulder under his right arm.

"Back to camp? Hot broth? Sleep?" Cassende suggested.

Ivvar's legs felt suddenly weak. He wanted all of those – camp, broth, sleep – right *now*. If only he didn't have to walk to them.

"Can you manage?" Pai asked him.

Ivvar grunted. "Do you know the direction?"

Cassende surveyed them, probably wondering if they were fit to go even the few hundred steps it would take to get there, but she answered. "I do. It's this way." She looked toward her right, then looked back at them. "We'll take it slow."

Cassende paused at the edge of the meadow where Paiam's tent stood undisturbed. The coals of the banked fire glowed, and the pale blanket of snow – soft under the moon – showed only the footprints made by herself and the two Hammarleedings. The encircling pines and the bluff stood like dark walls around the open expanse.

The fight between Ivvar and the wyrm had not passed through it. Nor had the ice spirit led the monster away in this direction. Balance be praised! She hadn't the least idea of how to set up Ivvar's tent. Or anyone's tent.

Cassende glanced over her shoulder. Paiam and Ivvar had fallen behind, limping with fatigue and Ivvar's injuries, each shoring the other up, but they were in sight. They'd make it here without her help. Not that her help would *be* much help. She wasn't short, not truly, but these Hammarleedings were both so tall.

She crossed the meadow briskly.

Add wood to the fire, start some water to boil, check that the tent was fully ready for occupants. Ivvar and Paiam had cared for her in her weakness. Now she would care for them.

The water was hot by the time Paiam and Ivvar stumbled to the fireside and fell more than sat on the waiting groundcloth. Paiam slumped against Ivvar's pack – retrieved en route to camp along with her trekking poles. Ivvar slumped against his own knees, bent up before him.

Cassende had found Paiam's bouillon pastilles and a tin bowl, in addition to the tin mug, in Paiam's pack, left inside the tent. Now she rummaged in Ivvar's pack for another drinking vessel. Ah, there was his mug.

The bouillon felt like rough salt, but slightly moist, as she crumbled it into the cups and the bowl. She remembered to use a rag to handle the kettle, but burned her forefinger when she started to pass a mug to Paiam.

Ouch! Crockery dishes didn't conduct the heat like that. She'd never used metal ones before. She plunged her hurting finger into the snow. Maybe it wouldn't form a blister.

Paiam had winced and now looked at Cassende, a rueful expression on her face. "You okay?"

Cassende nodded. "It's too hot to drink anyway."

Ivvar's eyes were closed. The firelight flickered on his weary face. Had he gone to sleep sitting up?

She and Paiam would never manage to get him into the tent if he had.

"'M alright," he mumbled.

So, no, not asleep.

He opened his eyes, more focused than before. "Did I say 'thank you'? I don't think I said it." He leaned forward to take Cassende's other hand – the one not plunged into the snow. "Cassende. Thank you."

Balance, but the man could muster intensity, even in the aftermath of a fight to the death!

She smiled. "I saved myself, too. And only after you rescued me. Twice."

He inclined his head, then turned to Paiam, gazing at her in a momentary silence.

He must love her, Cassende realized. She'd known almost from the first that they had to be friends. They were too comfortable to be merely acquaintances. Were they more than friends? Or had they been?

Ivvar broke his silence. "Pai, thank you isn't really enough."

Paiam looked as though she might have chuckled, if she hadn't been so tired. "We'll talk," she said. "In the morning."

"Yes." The fatigue returned to Ivvar's face.

Cassende checked her burned finger. No blister. Yet.

She tested the bouillon mugs – cooler – and passed them to her two companions.

She blew on her own serving in its tin bowl, then took a sip. Mmm. Salty, savory, and *good*. She hadn't realized she was hungry. She took another sip, and then gulped the rest down. It was filling, satisfying the empty feeling in her stomach.

She rinsed their dishes with the leftover water, then spread the bedrolls – two of them – inside Paiam's tent.

Ivvar crawled awkwardly through the tent flaps, clearly favoring his bruises.

Paiam paused, squatting a moment. "Do you need help setting up Ivvar's tent?" Fatigue smudged her eyes.

There wasn't room for three in Paiam's tent. Two was going to be a squeeze. And Cassende had never in her life set up a tent.

She looked Paiam serenely in the eye. "No. I'll manage fine." And she would; just not the way that Paiam imagined. Paiam sighed, shook her head, and crawled inside.

Cassende tied the tent flaps closed behind her and straightened to survey their camp: fire settling nicely, wood stacked nearby, packs re-packed and buckled closed, resting on the groundcloth. Everything tidy. Nothing amiss. She drew in a deep breath of the cold, fresh air. Unlike Paiam and Ivvar, *she* was not tired. She felt renewed, and the night was hers.

She stood still for another moment, taking it all in.

The moon shone high in the indigo sky, large and round and bright, obscuring the stars nearest while the others sparked like crystal. Were star-drakes anything like ice wyrms? She'd heard the legends as a child and assumed them solely the stuff of story. Now, she wondered.

The night air remained beautifully still and cold, while she stood warmly in Paiam's lent clothing, enjoying just being present for all this.

She exhaled, slowly, luxuriously, and felt her antiphony – safe magic, not the perilous troll-magic – stir in her core: root radix, belly radix, plexial center, heart, throat, brow, and crown. Faint ripples of harp music sounded, not in her ears, but in her antiphonic perception.

She turned her attention inward to discern . . . what might be there. What she wanted to be there. What she hoped would be there. What she'd glimpsed at the end of the titanic struggle with the wyrm.

Her radices, the sources of her antiphony, lay exactly where they should – anchored there – and held exactly their proper shapes.

Relief and rejoicing swelled within her.

It was true. She was no longer a troll. The *ilmatar* had healed her.

She could feel health and strength collecting within her bones and muscles, guided there by her newly re-attached radices. Troll-magic ripped an antiphoner's radices from their moorings, and each radix then drifted farther from its healthy configuration, yielding infirmity in body and mind. She had strayed into troll-magic to save her son. Now her error was redeemed.

The rest of her life lay open before her.

It was astonishing.

I'll see my children again. Perhaps meet my grandchildren, when they are born.

She contemplated her husband, remembering him in their last moment together: his eyes anguished, the torch-bearing mob at a distance behind him.

"Go! Go, Cass! I can't stop them!"

She'd gone, knowing her death by mob violence would destroy him. Had she left him to *his* death?

She'd thought so many times during her agonizing flight.

Now . . . she thought differently.

Her absence had freed him to preserve himself, not needing to devote his efforts to protecting her. He was a canny man, and able.

He's alive. I know he's alive.

She contemplated their future reunion till dawn.

～

Paiam woke up in the night feeling happy.

She lay on her side. Before her, the tent canvas – a sturdy weave of thistlesilk – glowed pale tan. The moon must still ride high in the sky, casting its full light over all below and shining through the tent wall. She could see the rumpled folds of the bed roll wrapping her so warmly.

The fatigue in her body had melted, and she felt gloriously relaxed, rested by her first interval of sleep.

Ivvar's solid length bulwarked her back. The tent was designed for one person and her gear, not two. Even leaving their backpacks outside, they'd had to lie close to fit. She'd barely noticed it when she climbed into her blanket and fell headlong into slumber. Now it felt good. Ivvar's arm had escaped his bed roll to encircle her waist.

She welcomed his sleeping embrace.

This was the way they were meant to be. Together.

Together in the daylight, tackling whatever the day brought.

Together in the night, sleeping close.

She shifted her head on the small knitted pillow beneath it. The strand of hair loosened in her *duoja-fight* with the wyrm strayed onto her cheek, tickling her skin. She extracted her top arm from the blankets to tuck it back. The air felt cool on her hand, and she hurriedly snuck it back into the warmth of the bedroll.

She felt Ivvar stir, snugging her in closer.

A slow smile curved her lips.

Somehow, without words, she and her former linking-brother had settled their differences. Perhaps because their differences were never those of opinion, to be resolved by arguing. They'd known how to compromise. They hadn't known how to work together as a team. *We needed to learn how to* act *in concert.* And the ice wyrm had taught them that.

Where will we go from here?

Somehow it didn't matter to her. She'd learned to trust the future instead of fighting it. She and Ivvar would always be friends, no matter how they arranged the details.

Perhaps they'd renew their linking-bond. Perhaps they wouldn't.

Perhaps he'd return to his old home, Tukeva-lodge. Perhaps he would continue to live in Rakas-lodge.

Perhaps they would follow the traditional pattern of seeing one another only on Hammarleeding fete-days. The men joined the women on all but one of them now, ten out of the eleven. Unlike the years of their linking, when the Tukeva-brothers visited Kaunis for three celebrations only.

Maybe they would do something crazy, like traveling on an extended wanderyar for the rest of their lives, sharing this tent. She bit back a laugh. No, better obtain a tent meant for two.

How might Ivvar feel about joining Minmahal-tribe, becoming one of the Reindeer People? Not only would they see each other every day, they'd see Livli and their great grandchildren as well.

Whatever they chose, it would be good.

The first time Ivvar awoke in the night, he groaned. Softly, so as not to disturb Pai, but oh, his whole body felt stiff and sore. Although . . . not nearly so bad as when he had crawled into his bedroll.

The deep pain of his bruises had passed off already.

This was the ache that came after heavy exertion, deriving from the miasma produced in the working muscles. He needed to move, that was what.

Could he wriggle out of his blanket without waking Paiam?

It was worth a try. He wouldn't be dropping off to sleep again if he just stayed put.

He drew in a deep breath, preparing himself to move.

And only then noticed the funk in the cold air. Ugh! That was him. All him. He hadn't bathed after his fight with the wyrm. And Paiam's part had been the extreme mental focus called for by *duoja*. Equally tiring, but not producing the sweat that moving the muscles required. She was not the source of the stink.

That decided him.

He inched his hands under him and levered his torso up to see the situation better. Paiam sighed in her sleep, but didn't awaken.

The tent flaps at his feet appeared to be tied on the outside. That was right; Cassende must have secured them, he and Pai too tired to remember. But the flaps at his head had been tied from the inside, not doubt when Paiam set up the tent in the first place. He would go that way.

He squinched further out of his bed roll. When the blanket fell to his waist, he extracted his legs. Gingerly to avoid knocking into his tent mate. Sitting up beside the tent flaps, it was a simple matter to undo the ties and slip out.

The snow chilled his bare feet abruptly. Apparently he'd managed to remove his short-hose and woolen boots before he slept. He didn't remember it.

But bare feet were merely a start. He intended to scrub down every part of him with handfuls of snow in the traditional Hammarleeding way. Usually that would follow sweating in the sauna. But not always.

He glanced around the meadow.

The moon still sailed high in the sky, brightening the pillows of snow on the trees and casting their limbs and trunks into sooty shadow. The fire had died, its coals coated with ash. A wink of amber showed itself, then vanished, evidence of retained heat.

Where was Cassende?

Ah, there on the ground cloth, gazing at the stars.

She looked down and caught his eyes. Her right eyebrow rose, questioning.

He cat-footed over to her.

"My clothes need changing," he murmured.

Her eyes widened a trifle. "You're feeling better? Your ribs?" She kept her voice low.

He grimaced. None of him felt truly good, but none of the aches were serious.

"Just sore. Moving will help."

She nodded, a rueful smile in her eyes. "I'll turn my back."

She did more than that, wandering toward the edge of the meadow to grant him a bit more privacy.

He doffed his tunic, leggings, undertunic, and undertrews with speed, tossing them in a pile on the vacated groundcloth. The bruises across his ribs showed black in the moonlight. Next came a few deep knee bends, slow push-ups, and the dawn-rising posture sequence of the Hammarleedings: stretch back, bend forward and place his hands on the snowy ground, lunge back with the feet, raise the hips, then lower them and raise the torso, and then the whole sequence in reverse.

It felt awful, every muscle screaming, but in a good way.

He repeated it twice more, glancing over his shoulder to be sure Cassende's attention was elsewhere. It was.

He was sweating when he finished. His muscles still ached, but they were warm and looser. He knew they'd be stiff again in the morning. Likely worse than stiff. But he'd do the dawn sequence again then. This was enough for now.

He grabbed a handful of snow and rubbed. It was shockingly cold, but a familiar shock. Face, neck, legs, arms, and all over his torso. He'd done this every day of every winter since he was a boy. It refreshed and cleansed, done thoroughly. He kept at it until his skin pricked out in goosebumps. Then he hauled fresh clothing from his pack and put it on.

"I'm done," he called softly to Cassende. She turned and waved, but stayed where she stood, staring into the woods. He frowned, then searched for his boots. Ah, there beside the tent. He collected them, sat on the groundcloth to brush the snow off his bare feet, and pulled on the footgear.

Cassende glanced over her shoulder as he approached her.

"The night is so beautiful," she said.

"Are you not tired? Shouldn't you sleep?"

"I'm not a troll any longer." Wonder sounded in her voice. "The *ilmatar* healed me."

Yes, he'd sensed something of the sort in the aftermath of the fight, but he'd been too battered to explore it more fully. He was glad for her. But he was still tired. A yawn cracked his jaws.

"You're welcome to my spot in the tent," he told her.

She reached out her hand to touch his. "The healing refreshed me. I need no sleep. Truly."

Perhaps that was just as well, because he did need sleep. A whole night of it, preferably.

"Call me if you grow weary."

Cassende's eyes smiled. "I will. Go rest, Ivvar."

Crawling in beside Paiam was sublime. Her blanketed, bony length felt familiar. And warm.

Another yawn stretched his jaws. Then he fell into sleep.

The cozy, dozy stage, when awareness persists in a dim way hovered around him for a time. The air in the tent smelled fresh now. His wool blankets, lined on the inside with thistlesilk, were soft. His skin was clean, his body, relaxed. Mm.

Then deeper sleep pulled him under.

Unaware, he lay bonelessly, comfortable despite the residual soreness in his limbs, soaking in the benefits of rest.

The tent grew dim, a small haven of dusky quietude, when the moon glided below the line of the tree tops.

Ivvar's second waking found him less alert than the first. He lay drowsing, conscious of Pai snugged in close, his right arm around her waist, his thoughts drifting. He could hear her soft breathing. The scent of the pear blossom oil she used in her hair rose to his nostrils, clean and sweet. This felt so right, so good, to be sharing sleep again.

We belong together, he thought. Would Paiam think the same?

He remembered her words to him after he'd brought Cassende back from hypothermia: "I'll never mind again."

He snorted softly. Yes, he rather thought Paiam did feel the same. But he'd ask her. No assuming anything, not this time. That had been part of their troubles in the past, that he assumed she felt the same as he. She hadn't. He could see that now. Their regular parting – the traditional pattern of Hammarleeding life – had been much more difficult for her than for him. He would always ask now, when they grew angry with one another. That was the only way to get to the heart of a difference. Without questions, you argued the surface problems, which didn't solve anything.

He opened his eyes, wanting to see Paiam's face.

The tent was very dim, and she lay with her back snuggled into his chest. The crown of her head reached to just below his nose. All he could see of her were the narrow braids of her hair, neatly running from her brow back across her scalp and then down to the nape of her neck where they gathered together in one lone, thick braid. During the day it encircled her elegant head like a coronet. Now, in the night, it lay over her shoulder, long and substantial. One strand of wooly gray strayed from the plaits above her forehead to brush her temple and cheek.

Ivvar propped himself up on his left arm.

Why . . . she was awake. And smiling.

She shifted her head to look at him.

His heart turned over. She was so lovely. The wisdom and serenity she'd gained with the years combined with her inner fire in a way that he found irresistible.

"Pai, will you share a linking-bond with me again?" The words fell from his mouth. He'd not meant to ask her so soon. He'd wanted to talk over what he'd learned, beg her forgiveness, ask her what she would like for their future. He thought she would approve of his idea that she join Illoiset. The sister-lodge shared the same slope above the lake as Rakas, his brother-lodge. Their lives would intertwine, day in and day out. There would be no partings. But he'd wanted to ask her about it before he proposed their linking.

Paiam's smile deepened. "I love you," she murmured, and then gave her answer, "Yes."

Ivvar leaned forward to kiss her cheek.

She lifted her face, and his lips met hers.

GLOSSARY

Brother A Hammarleeding man or boy.

Brother-lodge Hammarleeding men and boys live in all-male communities apart from Hammarleeding women. The term brother-lodge refers both to a community of males and to the large wooden chalet they inhabit.

Duoja A hero out of Hammarleeding myth, said to guard a sacred spring and to have vanquished warring demons. Her name is also used for the spiritual powers granted the Hammarleedings for healing, luring wild sheep down from the mountain peaks, and other purposes.

Father-lodge Brother-lodges are referred to as father-lodges when the speaker emphasizes the social and spiritual structures underpinning the community.

Frualte Lowlander honorific meaning "high lady." Remnant from the Hathorlynd occupation.

Ilmatar A nature spirit birthed by very cold ice.

Hammarleeding One of a reclusive people who live isolated in the Fiordhammar mountains.

Herralte Lowlander honorific meaning "high sir." A remnant from the Hathorlynd occupation.

Linking The Hammarleeding form of marriage is a celebration of their Mother Goddess, and the commitment to deity is emphasized over the commitment between the woman and the man. A couple might remain committed to one another for merely the duration of the ceremony, for a number of months or years, or for life. The bond between each parent and any offspring is permanent.

Linking-brother A woman's mate in the linking ceremony.

Linking-sister A man's mate in the linking ceremony.

Maitresse Giralliyan honorific meaning "Missus."

Mother-lodge Sister-lodges are referred to as mother-lodges when the speaker emphasizes the social and spiritual structures underpinning the community.

Motter Lowlander word for mother.

Patter Lowlander word for father.

Sister A Hammarleeding woman or girl.

Sister-lodge Hammarleeding women and girls live in all-female communities apart from Hammarleeding men. The term sister-lodge refers both to a community of females and to the large wooden chalet they inhabit.

Sweet-moon After a linking rite, some couples spend an entire month living together in a secluded moon-hut before parting to their separate lodge-homes.

TIMELINE FOR THE NORTH-LANDS STORIES

ANCIENT TIMES

Skies of Navarys..................3000 years before *Troll-magic*

THE BRONZE AGE

Resonant Bronze ....2000 years before *Troll-magic*

THE MIDDLE AGES

Hunting Wild ....800 years before *Troll-magic*

BEFORE THE STEAM AGE

Rainbow's Lodestone.......... ~100 years before *Troll-magic*

Star-drake........... immediately after *Rainbow's Lodestone*

THE STEAM AGE

Sarvet's Wanderyar ....52 years before *Troll-magic*

Crossing the Naiad ... concurrent with *Sarvet's Wanderyar*

Livli's Gift ....38 years after *Sarvet's Wanderyar*
(14 years before *Troll-magic*)

Troll-magic .... the now of this timeline

The Troll's Belt .... contemporaneous with *Troll-magic*

Perilous Chance .... contemporaneous with *Troll-magic*

Winter Glory.............................. 17 years after *Livli's Gift*
(3 years after *Troll-magic*)

J.M. Ney-Grimm lives with her husband and children in Virginia, just east of the Blue Ridge Mountains. She's learning about permaculture gardening and debunking popular myths about food. The rest of the time she reads Robin McKinley, Diana Wynne Jones, and Lois McMaster Bujold, plays boardgames like Settlers of Catan, rears her twins, and writes stories set in the realms of myth and legend or in her troll-infested North-lands.

Look for her novels and novellas at your favorite bookstore – online or on Main Street.

J.M. Ney-Grimm maintains a blog featuring flash fiction from her North-lands as well as other tidbits unearthed by her ever-active curiosity.

Visit her at http://JMNey-Grimm.com.